A Distant
Thunder

Raymond D. Mason

A Distant Thunder
Sackett Series Book # 9

Copyright © 2014 by Raymond D. Mason

All rights reserved. No part of this book may be used or reproduced by any means, graphic, electronic, or mechanical; including photocopying, recording, taping or by any information storage retrieval system without the written permission of the publisher/author except in the case of brief quotations embodied in critical articles and reviews.

Raymond D. Mason books may be ordered through authorized booksellers associated with Mason Books or by contacting:

You may order books through:
www.Amazon.com
www.BarnesandNoble.com
www.CreateSpace.com
www.Target.com

or personalized autographed copies from:
E-mail: RMason3092@aol.com

(541) 679-0396

This is a work of fiction. All characters, names, incidents, organizations, and dialogue in this novel are either the products of the author's imagination or are used fictitiously.

Printed in the United States of America

Preface

Life had been very difficult for identical twin brothers, **Brent** and **Brian Sackett** since the 'War Between the States' had found them fighting on opposite sides. Brent had gone off to help the South while Brian's sentiments lay with the North.

Brent Sackett had been hardened by the War. When the War ended Brent remained separated from the family, feeling they had slighted him with their allegiance to the North.

Through a number of incidents the two brothers had met briefly and even reconciled for a short time, but due to the law being after Brent he had to keep on the move to remain one step ahead of them.

Brent had met a woman he had fallen deeply in love with, but during a shootout with an outlaw gang she had been killed. The only thing that had kept him going was the fact that he wanted to finish the trip to California that he and his beloved wife had started.

We find Brent is still on his way to California, traveling with a ragtag accumulation of folks he'd met along the way who needed help. They are nearing Gila Bend, Arizona and looking for a few days rest from their grueling journey.

Brian Sackett had met and fallen in love with **Terrin Gibbons** when he and his oldest brother **AJ** rescued her and another man from a band of

Comancheros. As the two of them had gotten to know one another more, Brent believed that Terrin felt the same way about him as he felt about her.

A series of incidents at the ranch had kept him from spending as much time with Terrin as he would have liked and it eventually had an effect on her. Terrin had even made a move from San Antonio, Texas to the small town of Buffalo Gap, not far from Abilene, Texas where Brian lived.

Linc Sackett and his new business partner, **Clay Butler** started what they call a 'one horse rodeo' by buying a horse, that it appears, no one is able to ride. They travel from town to town betting cowboys they can't ride the horse. The two men found themselves in Tucson, Arizona where they hoped to make more money with their wonder horse.

Cheyanne LaFevre and her half-brother **Harmon** enter the story at this point. Harmon tried to steal a horse belonging to a rancher named **Clyde Johnson** but was caught by Johnson. A shootout occurred and Johnson's bullet grazed LeFevre's head. Johnson collected a small reward for LeFevre's capture.

1

**September 24, 1879
Territorial Prison
Leavenworth, Kansas**

Harmon LeFevre and Jeb Kenton lowered themselves over the prison wall to the ground below with a rope they had been making for over six months. They had managed to keep it secreted away waiting for the right time to make their escape.

This had been the night they had set a month earlier to make their escape. They overpowered one of the guards when he made his final round for the night. The two managed to get passed all of the other guards without being seen; that being a small miracle in itself.

Now that they were free they had to move quickly before they were missed. LeFevre had made arrangements to have two horses left in a grove of trees about a mile from the prison. Just as they reached the trees, the alarm at the prison sounded. It brought a chill to both men causing them to look back towards the prison.

"Thank God your sister brought the horses," Kenton said as they entered the small grove and saw the horses tied and waiting.

"I told you we could count on her," LeFevre said as they sprinted towards the horses.

"Why didn't she stick around?" Kenton asked.

"What? And be seen by someone. She said she'd leave them, but she wouldn't take a chance on anyone seeing her. She didn't want to get charged with aiding and abetting a prison break. Smart girl, my sister," LeFevre said.

When they arrived at the spot where the horses were tied, the first thing they noticed was the guns and gun belts draped over the saddle horns. Along with the gun belts were canteens filled with water. They quickly grabbed the gun belts and strapped them on before swinging into the saddle.

After mounting up Harmon opened the flap on one side of the saddlebags. He grinned when he saw the clothes his sister had put inside them. When he checked the other side of the bags he found food supplies; at least enough to get them to a town where they could get more supplies.

"She's thought of everything," Harmon said.

"Come on, Harmon they'll have the dogs out any minute now," Kenton said as he kicked his horse into a gallop.

"Head south, Jeb. We'll meet my sister in Wichita," LeFevre called out.

A Distant Thunder

The two men rode hard for over an hour before allowing their horses to rest. The animals were lathered and breathing heavy by the time they felt it was safe to slow them to a walk.

"We don't want to wind these animals in case they pick up our trail too soon," LeFevre said looking back over his shoulder into the darkness.

"They won't be able to follow us until it gets light enough to see," Kenton replied.

"That's what Bridges and Wallace thought, too...remember," LeFevre said with a slight frown.

"Let's change out of these prison rags and into the clothes your sister put in these saddlebags," Kenton said.

"Yeah, that's a good idea," LeFevre said, and then had another thought. "Wait a minute, Ben. There's a creek around here somewhere. Let's change clothes there and it will slow the dogs down a little and give us more of an advantage."

They rode about ten minutes more and came to the creek that LeFevre had remembered. They changed into the clothes supplied by LeFevre's sister and tossed their prison clothes into the creek. They allowed their horses to drink their fill and then headed on in the direction of Wichita, Kansas and the Bull's Head Saloon and Dance Hall.

Harmon LeFevre had served two years of the life sentence he'd received for his crimes. He had been sent to Leavenworth for desertion, for robbing a Wells Fargo freight office and shooting and killing a guard. He'd managed to get away with over three thousand dollars. LeFevre had robbed a stagecoach and shot and killed the man riding shotgun.

The man who had actually captured Harmon was a rancher by the name of Clyde Johnson. Johnson captured LeFevre by accident really, when Harmon tried to steal Johnson's horse after his had given out on him. Johnson had fired at LeFevre and the bullet had grazed his temple, rendering him unconscious.

After the sheriff had arrested LeFevre for trying to steal Johnson's horse was when he discovered the wanted poster that was out on LeFevre. The reward of fifteen-hundred dollars had gone to Johnson. This had occurred in Hays City, Kansas two years earlier.

Jeb Kenton was an Army deserter who had been serving twenty years in prison for killing three people. He had claimed self defense, but the truth was he'd ambushed the three cavalrymen before robbing them.

Due to the fact that he'd had a run in with two of the men a few days earlier and claimed he had deserted for fear of losing his life, the army board had gone easier on him. He'd only served a few months over five years when he decided to make the break with LeFevre.

The two men had become fast friends after LeFevre had saved Kenton from an attempted killing by another prisoner who had it in for him. The word had gone out to leave both men alone since LeFevre had surrounded himself with some of the hardest cases in the prison.

LeFevre had sworn to get even with the rancher who had caused his capture, and over the years his desire for revenge had only increased. Now that he was out he was bound and determined to find Johnson and kill him.

Harmon had told Cheyanne he wanted her to locate the rancher while he was in prison. To a man like Harmon revenge was the motivating factor in escaping. He'd make the man pay and pay dearly for bringing him down and getting him sent to prison.

Raymond D. Mason

2

Wichita, Kansas
September 30, 1879

It was nearing six o'clock in the evening, six days after LeFevre and Kenton had made good their prison escape, when they rode into Wichita, Kansas. They had laid false trails and back tracked to throw off any posse that might be pursuing them.

They asked the first person they met on the busy street to direct them to the Bull's Head Saloon and Dance Hall. The man told them it was about three blocks away but on the main street.

They found it with no trouble and tied up in front of the saloon. They took a long look up and down the busy street before stepping down off their horses and entering the building. Once inside they headed straight for the bar. When they reached it LeFevre motioned for the bartender.

When the bartender walked up to them LeFevre asked, "Do you have a singer here by the name of Cheyanne LeFevre?"

Raymond D. Mason

"Yeah, she'll be coming on to do her show in just about five minutes. You must be new in town," the bartender answered.

"We are...how'd you know?" LeFevre asked as he looked around the large room.

"The regulars know her schedule better than we do. She's something else, I'll tell you that," the bartender laughed and then added. "What'll it be, gents?"

"Beer...and keep 'em coming," LeFevre said and laid a silver dollar on the bar.

"You've got it, pardner," the bartender said as he turned and walked away to draw a couple of beers.

"It's been a long time, eh, Harmon?" Kenton said with a grin.

"Too long...to my way of thinking, Jeb," LeFevre said and then looked towards the front doors.

The Wichita sheriff and a deputy entered the bar and stopped, looking around the big room. LeFevre and Kenton instantly turned their backs toward the lawmen, but continued to watch them in the long mirror behind the bar.

The sheriff scanned the room until he saw who it was he was looking for and said something to his deputy. The two of them walked over to a table where three men were seated.

The sheriff spoke to one of the men and the man instantly got up and followed the two lawmen out of the saloon. LeFevre and Kenton watched and once the three men had gone commented.

A Distant Thunder

"Now I wonder what that was all about Harmon." Kenton said.

"I have a feeling the older gent may be a doctor. He picked up that little black bag that was sitting on the floor next to his chair. Someone must have had need for a sawbones," LeFevre said.

Just then the orchestra in front of the large stage struck up a tune and everyone's attention was diverted to the stage. The curtains pulled back and Cheyanne LeFevre came out of the wings.

She looked around the big room and then smiled, "Well, boys...are you ready for a good show?" she called out.

"Yeah, Cheyanne...let 'er rip," a cowboy yelled out.

With that Cheyanne went into her opening number. It was an upbeat tune that got everyone in the bar singing the chorus along with her. You could tell the young, pretty woman was enjoying herself.

She was almost to the end of her number when she finally looked in the direction of her brother and Jeb Kenton. Her demeanor changed slightly, but she quickly brought the smile back.

The truth was that Cheyanne had been reluctant to help her brother escape. She'd seen how much he'd changed over the years and didn't like it. Still, he was her brother and she hated the thought of him spending his best years in prison.

Cheyanne did two numbers and took a break. The management didn't want the customers simply watching her act, they wanted them drinking and gambling. That fact made her job a lot easier.

Raymond D. Mason

Cheyanne made her way through the admiring crowd to the bar where she greeted her brother and gave Kenton a slight nod. She smiled wanly as she said, "Hi, Harmon; I see you made it out okay."

"Yeah, thanks to you, little sister, Harmon said. "Hey, you were really good up there. You've got these guys eating out of the palm of your hand."

"It's a job and it pays well," Cheyanne said in a tight voice.

"Yeah," Harmon said, noticing her lack of enthusiasm as she looked from him to Kenton and then down at the floor.

"You don't act all that happy to see your big brother, sis," Harmon said.

"Harmon, did you hurt anyone making your escape?" Cheyanne asked with a frown furrowing her brow.

"We had to club a guard if that's what you mean," Harmon said in a taut voice.

"You didn't kill anyone, I hope," Cheyanne replied.

"No, we didn't kill anyone. Now back to my question to you. You don't seem too happy to see us," Harmon said.

"I'm your half-sister, Harmon, I've got a good thing going here and I don't want to louse it up. I did what you asked me to do and that's as far as I'll go. You said no one would be hurt in your escape and that you would be heading for California and I've got two tickets for you and...him...on the train that leaves tomorrow afternoon. I hope you'll be on it," Cheyanne stated firmly.

Harmon gave her a hard look and then grinned, "Yeah, we'll head out tomorrow. Did you find out where this Johnson fella lives?"

"He sold his ranch and moved out west. That's all I know and that's what I told you the last time I visited you. I haven't learned anymore than that," Cheyanne said.

"You mean you don't know where he moved to?" Harmon asked sharply.

"No, I wasn't able to find that out," Cheyanne snapped back.

"Never mind, I'll find out where he is and that's where I'll go. Why don't we get us a table and have a few drinks for old time's sake; what do you say?" Harmon said in an attempt to brighten the mood.

"I don't want to know about anything you might be planning on doing after you leave here, Harmon. I've done what I said I'd do and that's as far as I'll go," Cheyanne said honestly and firmly and then added.

"I'll have to do another set in about ten minutes and I have to change," Cheyanne said as she started to go.

"We'll be here when you're finished...you will join us, won't you little sister?" Harmon said firmly.

"Yeah...sure...whatever you say," Cheyanne said and turned and walked away from the two.

"Your sister doesn't seem all that happy to see us, Harmon. What's her problem, anyway?" Kenton asked.

"I don't know, but I can tell you this...I don't like it...I don't like it one bit," Harmon said as he watched his half-sister walk away.

"I'll tell you something else, Jeb," Harmon said with a smirk. "When we leave here tomorrow...she's going with us. She just doesn't know it yet."

3

Buffalo Gap, Texas
October 2, 1879

Brian Sackett reined his horse to a halt in front of Ellen Ellis Boarding House and sat there for a moment before stepping down. He had something he wanted to say to Terrin Gibbons that he'd been rehearsing all the way from the Sackett ranch to the small town of Buffalo where Terrin was now living.

"I hope you know how I feel about you..." Brian said quietly to himself and then shook his head negatively. "No, that's not right. Terrin, I want you to be my bride. I promise to love you with every beat of my..., no; that sounds like I'm a poet or something."

Brian stepped down out of the saddle and opened his saddlebag flap and took out a small bouquet of flowers he'd picked on his way there. He fluffed the pedals so they weren't so mashed down and then sniffed the fragrance of the bouquet.

He wiped the toes of his boots on the back of his pant legs and then moved up to the front door of the boardinghouse. He pushed the door open and peeked in. When he saw Mrs. Ellis he grinned. She was seated in the parlor with her knitting in her lap and her head down and her eyes closed.

Brian tiptoed in so he wouldn't wake the sleeping owner and started up the stairs. When he stepped on a creaking board Mrs. Ellis called out, "Who's there?"

"Oh, it's me, Mrs. Ellis. I was just going up to see Terrin," Brian called back.

"You come in here and say a proper hello to me," Mrs. Ellis said in her somewhat stern voice.

"I was going to, but I didn't want to wake you," Brian said.

"I wasn't sleeping; I was just resting my eyes," she replied.

"Oh, just resting your eyes, huh?" Brian said as he walked into the parlor.

"I'll save you a hike up those stairs, Brian Sackett. Terrin isn't up in her room. She has herself a new job. She just started it day before yesterday," Mrs. Ellis informed Brian.

"A new job you say?" Brian questioned. "Doing what?"

"She's the new clerk in the Cattlemen's Bank. She'll make a good one, too. That girl is as smart as a whip. Why, she'll probably be the bank president by this time next year," Mrs. Ellis laughed.

Brian checked the big grandfather's clock in the parlor and saw that it was 11:45 AM. He looked back at Mrs. Ellis and excused himself.

"You wouldn't know what time she gets off for lunch, would you?" Brian asked.

"It just so happens I do. She gets off at 12:00 on the dot," Mrs. Ellis said and then made a special note of the flowers in Brian's hand.

"Are those flowers for me?" Mrs. Ellis said teasingly.

"Uh, no, but next time I'll bring you some, too," Brian grinned.

"Yeah, probably a tumbleweed," Ellen said with a laugh.

"Excuse me for running off, but I've got something very important to discuss with Terrin," Brian said.

"I'll bet I know what it is and it has to do with church bells, doesn't it."

"It very well could," Brian said as he edged towards the door.

"Well, go on over to the bank. Don't let me hold you up since you ain't going to propose to me."

Brian chuckled as he tipped his hat and headed hurriedly towards the door. Once outside he swung into the saddle and trotted his horse down the street to the bank.

He had just tied up in front when the front shade was pulled down. He looked around and saw a clock over the drug store entrance. It was only 11:52. It was a might early for the bank to close, Brian thought to himself.

Something didn't seem right to the tall rancher and he decided to look around the corner at the other side of the bank building. He walked to the corner and peered around it towards the side door the employees used after closing time.

There was a man on horseback sitting near the side door and holding two other horses. Brian knew instantly what was going on. It was a bank holdup...and Terrin was inside with the holdup men.

Brian moved back out of sight of the man on horseback and pulled his .44 from its holster. He listened intently to see if he could hear when the men exited the bank. He didn't have to wait long.

Brian heard the door open and voices coming from the area where the man was holding the horses. He peered around the corner again and when he saw one of the men who had been inside the bank emerge, Brian stepped out into full view.

Brian raised his pistol and aimed it at the man holding the two horses. "Hold it right there," he called out as he cocked the hammer back on his pistol.

Before he knew what was happening the second man emerged from the bank, only he wasn't alone. He was holding Terrin in front of him as a hostage. He froze.

"One false move and she's dead," the man holding Terrin yelled out.

Brian moved back behind the corner of the building out of sight. He closed his eyes at the thought of Terrin being held as a shield for these bank robbers. He peeked around the corner again and saw the man who was holding Terrin lift her up so she was sitting behind the man who had been holding the horses.

A Distant Thunder

"If you want to be responsible for this young woman's death, follow us," the man who had dragged Terrin out of the bank yelled out.

"Don't hurt her; I ain't doing nothing to stop you," Brian called back to the man.

"We'll let her go when we're a mile out of town if we don't see anyone following us. If we do...we'll drop her dead body," the man called back.

Brian felt sick to his stomach. These guys meant business. He wasn't about to take any chances of Terrin getting hurt or possibly killed. All he could do then was watch them ride away with his intended.

Just then one of the bank's clerks run out the front door and began shouting, "The bank's been robbed...the bank's been robbed." Brian looked towards the man and then back in the direction of the now fleeing holdup men. He couldn't just let them take Terrin without making any effort to stop them.

Raymond D. Mason

4

Brian sprinted to his horse and mounted up. Instead of following after them, however, he rode parallel to their route of escape. Hopefully they'd be too busy looking behind them they wouldn't see him riding in the same direction they were.

The outlaws kept an eye out for anyone following them, but didn't pay all that much attention to either side. Brian managed to ride in arroyos and low spots so he wasn't as visible.

True to their word when the outlaws were a mile or so out of town the rider with Terrin on the back of his horse reined up. He gave her a shove that sent her sprawling to the ground. Without a single word the three men rode off, leaving their pretty hostage behind.

The bandits were out of sight before Brian got to where Terrin was just getting up off the ground. When she saw him she gave a huge sigh of relief. Brian rode up fast and hit the ground running. He stopped in front of her with eyes wide.

"Are you all right, Terrin?" Brian asked as he took her in his arms.

"Yes, I'm okay. Scared, but they didn't hurt me," Terrin replied.

"You're sure you're okay?"

"Yes, I'm sure, Brian. Let's get back to town. They pistol whipped Dan...Mr. Travers, the bank president. I'm afraid he's hurt really bad," Terrin said.

Brian helped her up into the saddle and he climbed on behind her. They made the mile or so ride back into town and went straight to the bank. When they arrived a large crowd had formed. The first person they saw was the sheriff of Buffalo Gap, Bob Payne.

When the sheriff saw Terrin he asked quickly, "Are you alright, Miss Gibbons?"

"Yes, I am Sheriff. How's Mr. Travers?" Terrin asked.

The sheriff looked down and then raised his eyes to meet hers, "I'm afraid he didn't survive the beating. The doctor just pronounced him dead."

"Oh no...oh no," Terrin said aghast at the sheriff's words, her eyes filling with tears.

Brian watched as Terrin's eyes teared up. He was sorry the bank president had died, but Terrin seemed to be taking the news extra hard. He figured it must be due to the fact that Travers had given her a job and she felt somewhat indebted to him because of it.

"Come on, Terrin, I'll take you back to the boardinghouse," Brian said.

"No, Brian...I want to stay here. I might be of some comfort to the others," Terrin said.

A Distant Thunder

The sheriff looked at Terrin and then at Brian and said, "Go ahead and take her home. We're sending all the employees home. The bank will be closed until further notice. The bank officials will have to select the next president and until that is done, the bank will remain closed."

"My deputy is getting a posse together and we're going after the bank robbers. We'll get 'em," the sheriff said firmly.

"Oh...," Terrin said as she looked quickly from the sheriff to Brian. "In that case, please take me home, Brian."

Brian led his horse as he walked the half mile to Mrs. Ellis's Boardinghouse with Terrin. She was quiet and walked with her head down most of the way. Brian didn't talk much, mainly he just watched her.

This ordeal had truly upset her. He figured it had brought back the incident she'd gone through when she was taken captive by the band of Comancheros just before they met. After all, it hadn't been that many months ago when that occurred.

When they reached the boardinghouse they went in, but stopped in the parlor and Terrin told Mrs. Ellis what had happened. Immediately Mrs. Ellis told them to sit down and she hurried in and made a pot of hot tea.

While she was in the kitchen Terrin opened up a little more about her feelings. It seems that the bank president, who was a bachelor, had expressed his admiration for Terrin and the two of them had been keeping company. The news was hard for

Brian to take and it showed on his face and in his eyes.

"I hope you're not too upset, Brian. I was going to tell you about Dan the next time we were together. I hadn't chosen him over you, I just felt I needed time to decide which one of you I loved the most," Terrin said as she rung the hanky she was holding in her hands.

Brain listened quietly and when she had finished making her confession, smiled ever so slightly. He looked around the room, but wasn't seeing anything as he gathered his thoughts together. After several tense seconds he said, "I guess I was surer of my feelings for you than you were of your feelings for me. As far as I was concerned there was no other woman for me."

"Please don't be angry with me. I never lost my feelings for you; I just needed time to make sure they were not just because you saved me from the Comancheros. My feelings for Dan were different than those I felt for you...and still do," Terrin said honestly.

"Look, I'll give you as much time as you feel you need to determine exactly what your feelings are for me. I've been considering taking a job as a railroad detective. You may have helped me make up my mind," Brian stated.

"A railroad detective," Terrin repeated. "When did you decide you wanted to work for the railroad?"

"When Jim Tyler told me I'd make a good detective. I'd be one of the detectives who investigate train holdups. If it would be best that

A Distant Thunder

we didn't see one another for awhile that would be a good way to make it happen. I'd be gone back east to start my training," Brian said seriously.

"Are you sure that's what you want to do?"

"I don't know, Terrin; not now anyway," Brian stated. "I just thought it would be a good move to make. Now it looks like it might work out for the best. You can have all the time you need to think things over without any influence from me," Brian said with a slight frown.

"You're angry, aren't you?"

"Yeah, I think maybe I am. I'm sorry about Travers, I really am, but you hit me with a ton of bricks and its set me back a little bit. But, hey...I've got broad shoulders, I can take it," Brian said with a slight edge to his words.

Brian wanted to lash out at someone, but certainly not Terrin. No, he was hurt and the hurt made him angry. He knew he would be no comfort to Terrin, not the way he was feeling inside.

"I guess I'll go and let you get some rest. I'll let you know what I decide about the job with the railroad," Brian said as he stood up.

"I'm sorry Brian, I truly am," Terrin said and then asked, "What was it you wanted to see me about today? Was it anything important?"

Brian looked down at her and after a moment shook his head negatively, "No, nothing important."

With those final words he turned and walked out the door. He strode to his horse and mounted up. He never looked back as he reined his horse

27

Raymond D. Mason

around and kicked it into an easy gallop as he rode away from the town of Buffalo Gap.

5

Tucson, Arizona
October 3, 1879

Linc Sackett and Clay Butler sat in the Crystal Palace Saloon, renamed after Crystal Bell and her partner Lawrence had won the forced auction of the saloon two weeks earlier.

When Crystal saw the two 'rodeo men' she smiled warmly as she walked towards their table. She gave a little half salute as she neared them and said, "How're my two favorite cowboys doing today?"

"Fine as Crystal," Linc said with a chuckle.

"Oh, you're good with the words," Clay said half mockingly.

Crystal laughed, "I like it. So what would you two like today?"

"We heard you are serving one of the best breakfasts in town and we came to check it out," Linc said and then looked around the large saloon.

"And, we sure do like what you've done to this place in such a short time," Linc then added.

"Thank you. I could see the potential in this place the moment we laid eyes on it. We're not finished, though; not by a long shot. Wait until you see what I have planned for the stage we're going to put in," Crystal said, the excitement registering in her voice.

"Where's the stage going to be?" Linc asked as he looked around the room.

"In the new addition we're going to add at the side over there," Crystal said and pointed to the right side of the room.

Linc smiled, "You mean you're going to have a 'show room' all by itself?" he asked.

"That's right. Some people don't want to be distracted from their gambling or their drinking, so we're going to arrange it so those who want to be entertained can do so and no one else will be disturbed," Crystal said with a grin.

"I like it," Clay said.

"Me too," Linc agreed.

"Now, let me take your orders for the best breakfast in all of Tucson," Crystal said.

The two men ordered a large breakfast and Crystal left to get their orders. They watched her as she walked away and Linc stated, "That is one fine woman, Clay. She would make someone a good wife."

"Yeah, but not us, Linc; we're rodeo men, remember? She needs a man who will remain in one place, not go traipsing all over God's country rodeoing," Clay replied.

"I know, I didn't mean me...and definitely not you," Linc said with a laugh.

A Distant Thunder

Just after Clay had made his remark, three shots rang out from the street in front of the saloon. Both men looked towards the door and then quickly at one another.

"It's a little early for people to be celebratin', don't you think?" Linc said as both he and Clay got up and moved towards the door to see what the shooting was about.

When they walked onto the boardwalk they saw a man lying in the street face down. Two men were burning leather down the street, heading out of town. Linc and Clay rushed to where the man lay and slowly rolled him over so they could see how bad his wounds were. The first thing they noticed was the star pinned on his shirt. It was Bob Bell, Tucson's temporary sheriff. He was dead.

People had already begun to come out of their shops to see what had happened. A few of the men came up to where Linc and Clay were and asked who the man was who had been shot. When they heard it was Bob Bell they were stunned.

The man who owned the gun shop nearby shook his head slowly as he said, "Bob's brother, Bill, will be coming to town; you can bet on it."

Linc looked at the man and asked, "Bill Bell is this man's brother?"

"Yep, and the whole town will know when he arrives," the man said.

Linc looked at Clay and opened his eyes wide as he asked, "You know who Bill Bell is, don't you, Clay?"

"If a person doesn't know...they ain't from around these parts."

Raymond D. Mason

Bill Bell was known far and wide as one of the fastest guns in Arizona. He'd been a gambler, a faro dealer, a hired gun, and a sheriff in New Mexico. He and his brother had been very close and it was a given that he'd want the men who'd gunned Bob down brought to justice...or dead.

"Looks like there'll be a hot time in the old town very soon," Clay said.

A doctor whose office was just down the street had heard the gunfire as well and hurried up to where he could get a better look at the body.

"Oh, my Lord...it's Bob Bell," the doctor said quietly under his breath and then knelt down and took Bell's pulse.

After a few seconds the doctor said, "He's dead. Does anyone know who did this?"

No one said anything for a couple of long tortured seconds and then a man near the back of the crowd spoke up.

"It was the Wrango brothers, Hutch and Wayne," the man said.

"It figures," the doctor said.

"I take it the brothers are known around here," Linc Sackett said.

The doctor looked at him as though he had two heads, "You must not be from these parts," he said.

"I've been to Tucson a few times, but I never heard of anyone by the name of Wrango," Linc replied.

"Hmm," the doctor said just as another man walked up. The doctor addressed him the moment he saw him, "Hiram, he's all yours now; there's nothing more I can do for Bob."

A Distant Thunder

Hiram Davenport was the local undertaker. He was a tall, slender, solemn looking man who some said had never smiled. The sour look on his face suggested they may very well be right.

Clay Butler held a serious look on his face that Linc noticed causing him to do a double take.

"Have you heard of the Wrango's, Clay?" Linc asked.

"Yes...I have. It's been a few years, but I remember them all right. They came to Cottonwood on a so called business trip once. My brother in law and I had a little run in with them in one of the saloons there. They're bad news, I can tell you that," Clay stated.

"Well, it looks like they won't be coming around here much after what they did today. And if Bill Bell shows up that will be more of a reason for them to shy wide of Tucson," Linc concluded.

"I wouldn't count on it, Linc. The Wrango's thrive on trouble. In fact, they go out of their way to cause trouble. When they're in the area it's like a distant thunder. You know a storm is on the horizon and all you can do is to wait for it to hit," Clay stated with a frown furrowing his brow.

"I'll steer clear of them and hope they steer clear of me," Linc said ending the conversation.

Just about that time Crystal walked to the Crystal Palace Saloon doors and called out to Linc and Clay, "Breakfast is ready."

Crystal had been in the saloon and although she had heard the shooting, didn't know what had happened. When she saw the man being carried away she asked, "What happened?"

"Two guys just gunned the deputy sheriff down," Linc stated as they walked up the three steps to the saloon entrance where Crystal was standing.

"Oh, no...I hate violence," she said, something that seemed odd seeing as how she was part owner of a saloon and was around it almost daily.

Once the undertaker had carted the sheriff's dead body off to the funeral parlor the crowd broke up and went back to what they were doing. Everyone felt, however, that this was just the beginning of what could be a trail of blood. Bill Bell would be coming to Tucson, of that they were all sure.

6

Near Gila Bend, Arizona
October 3, 1879

Brent Sackett rode back to the wagon and announced that he had just seen the town of Gila Bend from a high ridge.

"Gila Bend is dead ahead," Brent said with a smile. We should be there in a few hours," he said as he rode up alongside the wagon.

"Oh, that is the best news I've heard for the longest time," Cheryl Keeling said with a sigh. "This heat was about to get to me."

"I know what you mean. It won't be long and you can enjoy a nice cool bath in a real bathtub," Brent said with a smile.

"And I can enjoy a cold beer," Grant Holt said and gave a chuckle.

"I'll join you, Grant," Brent said and then grew more serious as he warned. "Remember, I am John T. Holt, your older brother, Grant. And, Mrs. Keeling, you are my wife. I'm sure they have wanted posters out on me from what happened in Tucson."

"We've got it...John T.," Grant said with a wide grin.

"We'll see how long it takes before you forget and call him by his real name," Cheryl said with a wry smile.

"Forget and call who by his real name?" Grant asked curiously.

"Brent...," Cheryl said before thinking and then saw the grins on Brent and Grant's face.

"Aha, gotcha," Grant said as he and Brent began to laugh.

"Okay, okay...I messed up. But, don't forget...we're the only ones here. Wait until we've got strangers around us and we'll see who messes up," Cheryl replied.

"You'll both do all right, I'm sure," Brent said as he turned in the saddle and looked back behind them.

The smile quickly faded from his face as he spotted the cloud of dust on the distant horizon. He didn't like to see clouds of dust like this because it could mean trouble. He hoped it was merely a cavalry patrol.

Grant noticed Brent's curiosity and tried to see what had caught his friend's attention.

"What is it, Brent?" Grant asked.

"I don't know. It's just a large cloud of dust behind us. It may not be anything, but it could mean trouble. We'll have to be ready for whatever it is," Brent stated.

"Brent why don't you ride off behind that nearest hill over there," Cheryl said pointing to a small knoll.

"No, I'll stay and see what it is," Brent replied.

All three of them kept an eye on the approaching dust cloud until what was making the dust was in full view. It was a cavalry patrol and they caught up to the wagon quite quickly.

As they rode up, the captain leading the patrol raised his hand for his men to halt. They reined up so they were just behind the wagon. The captain had ridden up alongside Brent who was riding next to the passenger's side of the bench seat.

"Howdy, folks," the captain said looking at Brent first and then at the two atop the wagon's bench.

"Howdy, Captain," Brent said with a half grin. "Who are you chasing?"

"We're looking for three deserters from the cavalry. They're hard cases and dangerous to anyone whose path they may cross. We're on our way to Gila Bend to see if the three men the sheriff notified us that he has locked up in his jail are our boys," the captain explained.

"Deserters, huh," Brent said tightly.

"We've been on the men's trails for four days now and they must be getting low on food and water. They're armed to the teeth though. One of the men is a big German man by the name of Klaus Hauser. He's probably the meanest of the three.

"Hauser killed the second in command at Fort Huachuca where he was being held in the guard house until he escaped. He also killed one of the guards at the guard house. Be very careful of him if you should happen to run across them," the captain explained freely.

"What about the others?" Brent asked.

"Jerrod Younger is the name of one of the other men. He's a tall man with a moustache and missing a tooth in front that he got knocked out when he opened his mouth to the wrong man," the captain stated and then went on.

"The third man is quiet; doesn't say anymore than he has too. His name is Quincy Talbot," the captain said as he began to take more of an interest in Brent's appearance.

"Have we met somewhere before?" the captain asked.

"I doubt it, Captain. I've moved around a lot, of course that doesn't mean we couldn't have met. Let's just say if we have met, I can't remember where or when," Brent said and then changed the subject.

"We might see you in Gila Bend, Captain; seeing as how that's where we're headed also," Brent stated.

"Yes, we just might run into each other again Mister..., I don't think I got your name," the captain said curiously.

"Oh, that's right, we didn't exchange names, did we," Brent said cautiously.

"I'm Captain Bradley Wilkes and you are?" the captain questioned.

"This is my wife, Cheryl and my brother Grant. I'm John T. Holt, Captain," Brent said easily.

A Distant Thunder

"Nice to make you folk's acquaintance. Well, we're in a bit of a hurry so we'll be moving on. Remember what I told you about the men we're looking for; they're dangerous men," the captain said with a tip of his hat.

He turned and stood up slightly in the stirrups as he called out loudly, "Troopers...forward, ho!"

With that they kicked their mounts into an easy lope and rode on. Brent looked at Cheryl and Grant and let out a huge sigh of relief before saying.

"Whew...I'm glad that's over. One thing good that came out of them being here is the ones they're looking for won't be," Brent said.

"Yeah, and you even got your new name right," Grant said with a grin.

The three of them laughed at Grant's remark and then Brent said, "When we get into Gila Bend we'll find a place to stay for the night and then rest up for a couple of days before striking out for Yuma and the California border."

What they didn't know at that time was that three men were watching them from a distant hilltop. The men were the deserters the cavalry detail had been trying to run down.

Jerrod Younger looked at Quincy Talbot and grinned, "Now I wonder what the blue bellies were talking to those folks about?"

"I'll give you odds that it was about three men who had deserted. What do you think?" Quincy replied.

"I'd say you're right. What do you think Klaus?"

"I don't care what they were talking to them about. All I know is that I'm hungry and want to eat," the German growled.

"You were born hungry and you ain't gotten any better since then," Younger said with a laugh and then added. "Come on let's go see my old friend who lives just this side of Gila Bend. We'll not only get something to eat, but he'll probably have a couple of women there, too. He usually does," Younger replied.

"I don't know about riding in so close to the cavalry patrol, Jerrod? Aren't you pushing our luck a little bit?" Quincy argued.

"I don't think so. The patrol is looking for us ahead of them, not behind them. No, we don't have anything to worry about as long as we don't let those folks in the wagon see us," Jerrod grinned.

7

October 4, 1879
Train depot
Phoenix, Arizona

Harmon LeFevre, Jeb Kenton and Cheyanne LeFevre stepped off the train and onto the platform in front of the train depot office. Cheyanne wore a disgusted look on her face as she walked along between the two men with her. She had literally been forced to come along with her step-brother and Kenton against her will.

The reason for Cheyanne being with them was because Harmon had lied to the owner of the saloon where Cheyanne had been performing and got her fired.

Harmon had also told Cheyanne that should they get caught he would tell the authorities that she was in on their breakout from prison. Knowing he wouldn't hesitate to drag her name into it, she had come along willingly.

They took a surrey provided by one of the hotels into town and registered under the name of Ted Harmon and party. Once they were in their rooms, Harmon and Kenton headed for the hotel bar. Cheyanne was told to stay in her room until they came back for her. She wasn't one to be ordered around, however, and once the two men were gone, Cheyanne saw her chance to high tail it out of town.

When they arrived she had noticed that there was another train leaving in one hour and she planned on being on it. What she had held from Harmon was that she had learned where the man he had promised to kill had moved to. It was Yuma, Arizona.

If she did nothing else she planned on warning the man. Once she had done that she would go on out to California and start her life anew. Hopefully she could find work singing in some of the finer gambling houses in the San Francisco area.

Cheyanne made sure that Harmon and Kenton had left the hotel before leaving the room. She went downstairs and told the hotel clerk that she wouldn't be staying the night and would like the money back that had been paid for her room.

The clerk was reluctant to give her a refund, but when Cheyanne told him she would file a complaint with the sheriff of Phoenix stating that she had found bed bugs in her bed and that was the reason she wanted a refund, he relented.

From the hotel Cheyanne went straight to the train station and found a place that would be concealed from view in case Harmon came looking for her.

LeFevre and Kenton stopped and looked around the hotel bar, but decided it was too quiet and moved on down the street in search of a saloon with a little more excitement.

The two men immediately spotted a high stakes poker game that they felt could give them a grubstake. Both men had learned how to cheat at cards while in prison and they were good at it.

"Shall we show these boys how the game should be played?" Harmon said to Kenton.

"Do you mean the way it's played in Leavenworth?" Kenton said with a wry smile as he pulled a special deck of cards from his pocket.

"That's what I meant to say all right," Harmon laughed and then added. "Let's wait and see the one who's waiting on the table."

They didn't have to wait long before a cute little barmaid walked over to the table where the game was going on, carrying a tray of drinks. She sat the tray down on the empty table next to the one with the game and moved around the table placing the drink each man had ordered in front of them.

When the barmaid was finished she looked at one of the men in the game and nodded ever so slightly towards the man seated directly across from him. The nod wasn't much of one, but it was caught by both Harmon and Kenton.

"Did you see what I saw?" Harmon asked.

"I did at that," Kenton answered.

"The two of them are working a scam and that will definitely help us out," Harmon said with a grin. "Come on, follow me."

The two men walked over to the bar where the barmaid was standing with her back towards the room. One man walked up on her right and the other on her left side.

"So, little lady, I wonder what would happen if the others in the game over there found out that you and your partner are running a scam on them," Harmon said, coming straight to the point.

The young woman looked around quickly; first at one and then at the other before finally saying, "I don't know what you're talking about."

"Ah, come on now. We saw you clue your man as to who had the top hand over there just now. It's my guess that you tip him off every time you serve them drinks, which he will make sure is on a regular schedule," Harmon stated giving her a hard stare.

Now she began to show nervousness for the first time. Her head moved quickly back and forth between the two men who had spotted her and her boyfriend's con game.

"What are you planning on doing?" she asked tightly.

"Nothing...if you cooperate with us, but if you don't then we'll have to have a little talk with the management, as well as the men at the game," Harmon said with an engaging grin.

She grew silent for a few moments and then said, "What do you want me to do?"

"That's a good girl. It's very simple. When I get in the game I'm going to ask you to bring us a new deck of cards. You will, but you will bring this deck of cards," Harmon said as he handed her a sealed deck of cards.

She looked at him for a moment and then nodded her head okay. Harmon handed her the cards and gave her a grin. She stuck the cards in a small pocket on her apron and then spoke.

"I'd like for my boyfriend to get out of the game before you get in it," she said quietly.

"Well now I don't know about that. It seems to me he has most of the money at that table. So if he leaves he takes the money with him, doesn't he?" Harmon said unconcernedly.

"You know what to do, woman; now just do as you're told and you and your boyfriend won't have any problem. Don't do what you're told...and you won't have a boyfriend and you might go to jail for cheating those guys in the game over there," Kenton stated harshly.

The barmaid sensed that these two men meant every word they had said and figured the smart thing to do would be to go along with them. Harmon and Kenton walked over to the table where the game was in progress and stood there watching.

The young man working the con game with the barmaid looked up at Harmon and grinned as he asked, "We have an open chair if either of you'd like to sit in."

The other men nodded their agreement and Harmon looked at Kenton and said, "I'll sit in, if it's all right with you?"

Kenton nodded his okay and Harmon sat down. Because of Cheyanne having had some savings, Harmon felt he had enough to work his magic with the marked cards he would soon be delivered by the barmaid.

Kenton instantly moved over and ushered the young woman over towards the table. Harmon looked at the other gentlemen and said, "Do you gents mind if we get a fresh deck of cards?"

No one minded, even saying that doing so might change their luck. Harmon called out to the young woman, "Hey, honey...would you mind getting fresh deck of cards for us?"

The young woman cast a quick look at Kenton and then said, "Yes, I'll be right there."

She made a quick trip to the bar where she pretended to grab a deck of cards from behind it. While she was doing that Harmon took the opportunity to introduce himself to the other players as Hoyle Carson. The barmaid carried the cards back to the table and handed them to Harmon.

He pretended to tear the seal off the deck of cards and then asked who would like to shuffle. They said he could if he'd like since it was a new deck. He happily obliged them.

Kenton slipped on a pair of glasses that would pick up the markings on the marked cards and stood where he could signal the player's hands to Harmon. LeFevre soon had a nice pile of chips in front of him.

The boyfriend of the barmaid was fit to be tied at the sudden turn of events. She announced to the table that her boss wanted her to wait on a special game that was going on in an upstairs room and wouldn't be back. Another waitress would be taking their order.

Harmon and Kenton were so wrapped up in their winning that they lost track of time and before they knew it the hour was late. Late enough in fact that the train had pulled out for Yuma with Cheyanne as one of its passengers.

Raymond D. Mason

8

It was well past midnight when Harmon and Kenton returned to the hotel. They stopped in the hotel bar for one last drink before turning in. They had managed to bilk the unsuspecting gamblers for over a thousand dollars.

While they were in the bar, the hotel clerk that had checked them in entered and took a seat near them. He had just gotten off duty and always had one drink before heading home. When he noticed them seated next to him he spoke.

"Howdy, gentlemen," he said.

Harmon and Kenton recognized him as the hotel clerk and nodded their acknowledgment, but didn't make an attempt to engage him in conversation. That didn't stop him, however, from voicing his displeasure with the behavior of the young woman who had checked in with them.

"I hope you two are not as contentious as your female companion was earlier this evening," the clerk said.

Harmon looked at him coldly and replied, "What about her?"

Raymond D. Mason

"She checked out and demanded I refund the money for her room, that's what," the clerk stated.

"She checked out?" Harmon said, his voice registering his anger.

"That she did. She claimed there were bed bugs in her bed. I went up and checked and there wasn't one bug of any kind in that room," the clerk said.

"Where'd she go?" Harmon snapped.

"I have no idea where she went, nor do I care. The last I saw of her she was headed down the street towards the train depot. Perhaps she caught the late train out, I don't know," the man stated.

"Come on Jeb, we've got to find her...and quick," Harmon said jumping to his feet.

The two of them rushed out of the bar and out onto the street and towards the train depot. When they arrived there they found the last train for that night had already pulled out.

They went to the board that had the daily schedule posted on it and saw that the last train out; the one Cheyanne would have had to have taken went to Yuma.

"There's only one reason she'd be going to Yuma," Harmon snapped. "She went there because that's where the rancher is; I know her too well."

"She said she didn't know where he had moved to. Didn't she say she thought it was out to California?" Kenton questioned.

"If she went to Yuma, that's where he is. You don't know the gal like I do, Jeb. She's one of those goody two shoes that tended to hurt animals when we were growing up. She'd see a rabbit or even a fox that had been injured and she'd always want to nurse it back to health.

"I'd let her keep it long enough to get attached to it and then I'd either let it go free or kill it. Of course, I'd always give her some cock n' bull story to keep me in the clear," Harmon said with a smirk.

"And she never caught on, huh?"

"Naw, she was as gullible as my ma was. Now Pa was a different breed of cat all together. No one pulled the wool over his eyes. I tried a few times and felt the sting of his leather belt on my bare back," Harmon said with a frown.

"So what are we going to do now?" Jeb asked.

"We're going to Yuma. I've got a rancher to kill there by the name of Clyde Johnson," Harmon stated.

2:10 am
October 5, 1879
Abilene, Texas

The owner of the Red Dog Saloon looked at his only customer still in the bar and shook his head. The man was seated at a table near the back, slouched in a chair with a dour look on his face. He checked his pocket watch with the large clock behind the bar and then turned to his bartender.

"You can go on home Charlie. I'll lock up; once I get Sackett out of here, that is," the owner said.

Just then Brian Sackett downed the last of his whiskey and called out in a loud voice, "Bring me another shot."

"It's closing time, Brian. You'll have to get your drink somewhere else. Try that new place down the street, the Hog's Head Saloon. They never close," the owner stated.

"I don't want to go down there. I want to do my drinking here," Brian said, slurring his words slightly.

"Why don't you go on home? You've been here for nine hours. Go home and get some rest and come back tomorrow...which is today," the man said checking his watch again.

"You don't like my company, Joe? Is that it?" Brian said with a frown.

"That's not it. I'm tired and I'd like to close up so I can get some sleep. That's what you need, too; sleep. Now come on, I'm locking up," Joe said.

Brian rolled his eyes, but sat there for another few seconds before finally showing signs of getting up out of the chair. When he did get to his feet he was a bit unsteady, weaving back and forth slight.

"You won't see me in this place anymore," Brian said as he staggered towards the doors.

"You'll be back. In fact, the first drink when you come back will be on the house; how's that?" Joe said.

"I don't take handouts. I'll find another place to do my drinking," Brian mumbled.

Once outside Brian stood in front of the saloon and tried to focus his eyesight as he looked up and

A Distant Thunder

down the street. When two drunken cowboys exited the Hog's Head Saloon a block away, Brian headed in that direction.

He crossed the street and staggered through the saloon doors. There were half a dozen patrons in the saloon and two gals who served drinks along with one bartender. Brian flopped down in a chair at the first table he came to and called out loudly, "Whiskey."

"Hold your horses, cowboy," one of the barmaids said as she looked in his direction.

Brian looked all around the room until he spotted a portrait of a woman at the far end of the saloon. The portrait reminded him of Terrin which brought a deep frown to his face. He looked away quickly and slowly shook his head negatively.

"She done me wrong," he said to himself and paused before saying it louder, "She done me wrong."

Several people looked in his direction and one of the men in the place recognized Brian. The man, who was well on his way to being drunk, had once had harsh words with Brian over the sale of a horse.

"Hey, if it isn't the old horse thief Mr. Brian Sackett," the man called out. "How're you doing 'horse thief'?"

Brian slowly turned his bleary eyes towards the man and squinted as he tried to focus on the man's face. When he couldn't he pulled himself to his feet and weaved his way across the room towards the bar where the man was standing.

"What did you call me?" Brian asked as he approached the man.

"Horse thief," the man repeated.

"You'll take that back," Brian said.

"Or you'll what?" the man questioned.

"Or I'll shove my fist down your throat," Brian said.

The man wasted no time in throwing the first punch. He hit Brian a hard right to the jaw which knocked him backwards a couple of steps. Brian took a swing at the man, but was out of range and the swinging motion caused him to lose his balance.

The man moved up closer and drew back to hit Brian again when one of the barmaids hit the man over the head with a whiskey bottle. Due to the fact the bottle was nearly full the man was knocked unconscious and fell to the floor in a heap.

"Get those drunks out of here," the bartender yelled out.

"One of the men who had been standing with the unconscious man started to help him up. As he was pulling his friend to his feet one of the barmaids said to the bartender, "I'll take care of this one," she said as she looked at Brian who had sat down in a chair.

"Come on, cowboy...you can sleep it off in my room," the woman said as she took Brian's hand and pulled him to his feet.

"I want a drink," Brian said as he was pulled along by the woman.

She reached over and took a half full bottle of whiskey off the bar as they passed by it and continued on to her room on the second floor. Brian stumbled along after her, not really aware of where he was going.

"You'll feel better in the morning, cowboy," the woman said as they reached her room and she opened the door.

"I want a drink," Brian muttered.

"You've had a snoot full, all ready. You need sleep is what you need," the young woman said.

"Give me that bottle," Brian snapped.

"Okay, okay...drink your fool self to death for all I care," the woman said and handed Brian the bottle.

Brian uncorked the bottle and took a long slug of the whiskey. It was just enough to cause him to pass out. He fell across the woman's bed; out like a light.

"I'd hate to have your head in the morning, cowboy," the woman said as she removed Brian's boots.

"Looks like we're going to sleep crossways in the bed...doesn't it?" she said with a chuckle.

Raymond D. Mason

9

Brian awoke and looked around the room, not knowing where he was for several seconds. He looked at a small clock on a night stand and saw that it was 9:10. Brian squinted against the sunlit room as he tried to remember how he'd gotten here in this room.

He looked at the full sized bed he was in and noticed that someone had been in bed with him, but obviously wasn't there now. He slowly got out of bed and saw his pants hanging on the bedpost at the foot of the bed, with his shirt atop them.

Brian vaguely recalled walking up some stairs with a woman, but wasn't sure if it had actually happened or he made merely dreamed it. Just then the door opened and the pretty barmaid entered carrying a tray with a pot of coffee on it and two cups.

"Well, look who is back in the land of the living," she said with a warm smile.

"How'd I get here...who are you?" Brian asked.

"I brought you here after I saved you from a whooping you were about to receive at the hands of Butch Crowder. Don't you remember the fight?"

Raymond D. Mason

Brian touched his jaw and grimaced slightly, "Yeah, somewhat."

"Anyway, you were pretty well out on your feet, so I brought you up here to my room and let you sleep it off," she said as she sat the tray down and poured two cups of coffee.

Brian looked towards the bed and then back at the woman. She followed his gaze and answered the question he hadn't asked yet.

"Yes, I slept in the bed with you...and no, nothing happened. You went out like a light, but at least you didn't keep me awake with your snoring, because you didn't snore," she said with a chuckle.

Brian realized he was standing there in his long johns and quickly grabbed his pants and held them in front of him. The woman laughed at his shyness and held her coffee cup to her lips as she said, "Don't worry; you ain't got anything I ain't seen before."

"Maybe not, but you ain't seen mine," Brian replied as he hurriedly slipped his pants on.

The woman handed him his cup of coffee and grinned a friendly smile as she bit her lower lip. Brian gave her a studious glance and then asked, "What's your name?"

"Lacee Lawton...Brian Sackett," she said.

"How do you know my name?" Brian asked quickly and took a sip of his coffee.

"The man who gave you that bruise on your jaw called it out when you announced to the whole saloon that someone had done you wrong," Lacee said.

"Oh, I was a little loud, huh?" Brian said showing some embarrassment.

"A little...but hey, this is a saloon. Who isn't loud in a saloon," Lacee replied. "Would you care to talk about it?"

Brian looked at her and then slowly shook his head no, "No, it's nothing important and nothing you'd be interested in hearing, I'm sure," Brian stated.

"Try me. I'm a good listener," Lacee said flashing that warm smile again.

"I'm sure you are, but really, it's nothing. I was just a little down in the mouth last night and had too much to drink," Brian said and took another sip of coffee.

"Would you like some breakfast?" Lacee asked.

"Let me take you to breakfast," Brian replied. "It's the least I can do for you putting me up for the night."

"Oh, and the cowboy is a gentleman, as well," Lacee said with a chuckle. "I would be honored to have breakfast with you, Brian Sackett."

"Let me finish getting dressed and tell me where you would like to eat," Brian said as he grabbed his shirt and slipped it on.

"Right across the street is the best place for breakfast," Lacee said.

Brian washed his face and used one of Lacee's combs to comb his hair and the two of them went across the street to the café Lacee had suggested. They took a seat by the window and after the waitress had taken there order Brian glanced out towards the street. His eyes widened a bit when he saw his pa and brother AJ ride up.

"Oh, boy," Brian said under his breath, but Lacee caught it.

"Something wrong?" she asked.

"Yeah, my pa and brother just tied up out in front and are heading towards the door. I'm sure they'll want to know why I didn't come home last night," Brian said as he watched the front door.

"Don't' worry, I'll just tell them you stayed with me," Lacee said and watched Brian's reaction.

Brian looked quickly at her and then saw the slight grin on her face. He laughed and nodded his head slowly.

"You're a brazen hussy, I must say," Brian said with his own grin.

"Oh, Brian...that's the nicest thing you've ever said to me. I'm a brazen hussy," Lacee laughed.

Brian could tell she was a good natured woman and obviously had a kind heart. She certainly was pretty enough. He still wasn't sure just what kind of life she led, though; other than working as a saloon girl, that is.

John and AJ Sackett entered the café and looked around for an empty table. When they looked in Brian's direction a look of relief came to John's face; a look of surprise came to AJ's. They walked over to where Brian and Lacee were seated.

"Well, I'm glad to see you're all right, Brian. We were worried about you," John said and then looked at Lacee.

"Yeah, I'm fine, Pa. Meet Lacee Lawton," Brian said motioning towards Lacee. "This is my pa and this is my brother AJ."

"Nice to make your acquaintance," Lacee said cheerily.

"Same here, Miss Lawton," John said.

"Me too," AJ chimed in with a smile.

"I know you're wondering what happened to your son, so I'll tell you. He had a little too much to drink last night and I allowed him to sleep it off in my room. You have a perfect gentleman for a son here, Mr. Sackett," Lacee said evenly.

"I'm glad to hear that," John replied.

"I'll tell you so you don't have to ask. I work in the saloon across the street serving drinks to wayward cowhands like your son. When I see one who might be heading for trouble I try to head him in the right direction," Lacee said with a slight smile.

"I'll have to remember that," AJ said with a big grin.

Lacee laughed at AJ's remark. All three men could tell this woman was very comfortable with who she was and what she was all about. She was truly a likeable person.

Brian quickly added, "Won't you join us. We just ordered."

"No, we'll take a seat over there and let you two be alone," John said, sensing that there had to be something going on here that he didn't want to interrupt.

AJ, however, hadn't figured it that way. He was all too willing to take a seat. When John said they'd take another table it was easy to see AJ's disappointment.

The two of them excused themselves saying how pleased they were to meet Lacee and moved to another table. Lacee watched them go and then turned her attention back to Brian.

"You have a nice family from what I can see," she said.

"I like 'em, that's for sure," Brian replied.

"Do you have anymore brothers or sisters?"

"A bunch," Brian said. "Maybe you'd like to come out to the ranch sometime and meet some of them?"

Lacee turned her head slightly and cocked one eyebrow, "Are you asking me for a date, Brian Sackett?"

Brian grinned and said in almost a surprised voice, "Yeah, I guess I am."

"Then...it's a date," Lacee answered.

10

October 5, 1879
Gila Bend, Arizona

Brent Sackett gave the sheriff of Gila Bend a long, hard look as the sheriff questioned them on the subject of where they had been and where they were headed. He didn't like the attitude the sheriff was exhibiting in the manner of his inquiries.

Finally he'd had his fill and let the sheriff know it, "Hey, if you've got a problem with us passing through this one horse town of yours, say it. You have no call to talk to us like we're scum and you'd best change your tone of voice," Brent snapped angrily.

"Are you sassin' me, stranger?" the sheriff asked with a frown.

"Call it what you will, but you have no call to talk down to us like you've been doing ever since you walked up to us. Now if you have any questions we'll be glad to answer them, but not if you use the tone of voice you've been using," Brent said; his words tight and clipped.

"It looks like we've got us a regular hard case here, doesn't it Fred," the sheriff said to his deputy.

"This old boy must be the toughest hombre this side of the Mississippi River," the deputy replied with a smirk.

"Look, we told you where we were from and where we're going. If you have anymore questions you'll have to get 'em from someone else, because my well of information just ran dry," Brent said.

The sheriff glared at him for several long, silent seconds and then turned as if to go. Brent sensed the sheriff was about to try and hit him with a 'sucker punch' and stepped backwards one full step.

The sheriff suddenly swung around to throw a punch, but saw that he wasn't close enough for it to land. With his fist reared back, his eyes grew wide as he realized he had tipped his hand. Before he knew what was happening Brent threw his own punch which landed flush on the sheriff's jaw and knocked him to the ground.

The deputy started to pull his gun, but Grant beat him to the draw and held his gun on the man. The sheriff got to his feet wiping the blood from his nose as he stood up.

The sheriff let out a yell as he rushed towards Brent. Brent stepped quickly to one side and hit the sheriff another hard right to the temple area. The sheriff hit the ground again, this time a little more addled.

Several people had been watching the goings on and now were forming a semicircle to watch the

A Distant Thunder

fight. One of the men who had been watching the entire confrontation was the mayor of Gila Bend.

Brent let the sheriff get to his feet and wipe his nose again. Seeing more blood, the sheriff went for his gun, but Brent was much to fast. The sheriff stopped with his pistol halfway out of its holster.

"I think this has gone far enough," the mayor called out from where he was standing.

Brent turned and gave him a hard stare, "Tell him that," he said.

"I stood right here and watched this whole thing unfold and you folks can go. I want to talk to the sheriff alone. Jacob, you and Fred come to my office where we can sort a few things out," the mayor said to the sheriff.

"You're just going to let this bunch go after seeing what he did to me?" the sheriff said angrily.

"That is exactly what I am doing. That man was right in what he said to you. You talked to them like they were trash and I won't have that in my town," the mayor said.

"Your town, Mayor?" the sheriff snapped. "So just when did this become 'your town', I'd like to know?"

"The moment I took the oath of office administered by the town council," the mayor replied. "You have tried to run roughshod over everyone in town, but I'm calling a halt to it right now. From now on things are going to be run a little bit different," the mayor said tightly.

The sheriff glared at the mayor and then looked over at his deputy. The two of them locked eyes as if trying to send a message from one to the other. They were both men of the same mindset.

"I'll be over to your office in an hour or so," the sheriff stated as he turned to walk away.

"You'll come over there right now, or I'll take that badge from you here on the street," the mayor said firmly.

The sheriff stopped in his tracks and slowly turned back to face the mayor.

"You'll do what?" the sheriff asked with a frown.

"Come with me or give me your badge. I'm fed up with your bullying tactics and I'll have no more of it," the mayor said tightly.

"You listen to me you mealy mouthed, tin horn politician. I'll come and go as I see fit and that means to your office or mine. You're not going to tell me what to do and you certainly ain't man enough to take this badge away from me. I suggest you go back to your office and I'll come over there when I get damned good and ready," the sheriff said, almost spitting out the words.

The mayor stared fixedly on the sheriff as the two lawmen turned and walked in the direction of the sheriff's office. With clenched fists the mayor said under his breath, "Temper, temper, temper."

The truth of the matter was that the sheriff had run the town as though he was the boss and no one had a say in anything he did; whether it was legal or not.

The mayor had been elected because of his promise to clean up the situations that the sheriff

A Distant Thunder

had either failed to clean up or had played a major role in creating in the first place.

The two men had been heading for a showdown with one another for months, ever since the mayor had taken office. He had won in a special election when the previous mayor had been gunned down in an alleyway as he exited one of the town's brothels. It was suspected that it was in retaliation for a business deal gone sour. The other man involved in the soured business deal was none other than the sheriff.

The mayor walked briskly back to his office, but made four stops along the way. He stopped at the general store, the blacksmith shop, a hardware store and the newspaper office. He had the three owners of those businesses, who were members of the town council, follow him in order to be a part of what was about to take place. He was going to fire the sheriff.

"You're going to fire Jacob?" the smithy asked.

"And Fred…they're both going. One is as bad as the other and I'll not have two men of their character as part of the town's leadership," the mayor replied.

"I hope you have someone in mind who can take their place in the interim," the owner of the owner and editor of the Gila Bend Gazette stated.

"I do. Me," the mayor said flatly.

"You…?" they all questioned. "Have you ever been a sheriff or a lawman? Can you handle a gun?" the smithy asked.

"As well if not better than most as far as handling a gun is concerned. You had to be when

67

Raymond D. Mason

you were a deputy sheriff in Wichita. Anymore questions?" the mayor answered.

"You never mentioned that in your campaign speeches when you ran for mayor," the newspaperman stated curiously.

"I didn't think there was a need to do so. I was running for mayor, not sheriff. If you want to check on my references I can show you several newspaper clippings. If you want more proof than that I'll give you a demonstration of the fine art of handling a six shooter," the mayor said.

The five men waited for another forty minutes before the sheriff and his deputy showed up. They entered the office, obviously carrying a chip on their shoulder. When they saw the other four councilmen in the room, their demeanor changed somewhat.

"So what do you want to talk to us about, Mayor?" Sheriff Flagg asked.

"I want the badges you're wearing," the mayor said evenly.

The sheriff looked from the mayor to the four men seated around the room. He gave the men a smirk and then returned his gaze towards the mayor.

"It took me a long time to get this town just the way I want it, and I'll not let the likes of you four change that for me. If you want this badge you'll have to take it off me yourself. But, let me warn you; I don't like anyone touching my badge," the sheriff stated.

"That goes for me, too," Fred Banks said.

A Distant Thunder

"Then I guess that leaves it up to me to take them," the mayor said evenly.

The mayor got up and walked over to Sheriff Flagg and unpinned the badge from his shirt while looking directly into the man's eyes. When he'd take the sheriff's badge he turned and did the same thing to Fred Banks.

Neither man did anything when their badges were removed, but did stand there with slight grins on their face. The sheriff had noticed, however, that the mayor was now wearing a gun and gun belt and had the holster tied to his leg to promote a faster drawing of his pistol.

When the mayor had walked back behind his desk and was standing in back of his chair, ex-sheriff Jacob Flagg and ex-deputy Fred Banks went for their guns.

The mayor's hand was a blur as he whipped out his Colt and fired two shots. The first shot hit Flagg in the hand and the second shot hit Banks in the shoulder. Neither man had gotten a shot off.

The other members of the town council stood there in stunned silence. They'd seen some fast draws in their days, but they had never seen anyone as fast as their mayor.

The mayor looked at the two men he'd just wounded and shook his head negatively, "Now I'll have to arrest you two for trying to shoot me."

Flagg's thumb had been shot off which had him clutching his wounded hand against his stomach due to the pain and the bleeding. Banks was holding his shoulder with his good hand and looking wide eyed at the mayor.

In agony Banks managed to ask, "Where'd you learn to draw and shoot like that?"

"In different places, Fred," the mayor said. "I learned to draw fast and shoot straight when I was a young man fighting for the South. Later on I was a deputy to the Ford County under Sheriff, Bat Masterson. I also served for a short time as a deputy sheriff alongside Wyatt and James Earp."

"I need a doctor," Flagg said with a grimace.

"Me too," Banks agreed.

"Gentlemen, I'll see these two over to the doctor's office and then we'll discuss who might be our next sheriff. Like I said, I can take the job until a permanent sheriff can be found, then I'm back to being the mayor," the mayor said.

The blacksmith looked at the mayor with a wide grin on his face, "A sheriff is a lot more important than a mayor,"

"And it's a lot more dangerous than being a mayor, also," Mayor Haynes said.

11

The cavalry detail rode out of town back towards Fort Huachuca. They had been on the trail of the three deserters for five days, but had lost there trail shortly before arriving in Gila Bend. They had lost the horses' tracks in the rocks and had been unaware that the three had doubled back on them.

Now the three deserters could move about freely without being afraid of being spotted by someone who knew them. The first thing they did was head for a saloon. It just happened to be one that Brent and Grant had gone to earlier for a couple of beers.

The town of Gila Bend was abuzz about the mayor shooting the sheriff and his deputy and hauling them off to jail. The thought of it brought a grin to both Brent and Grant's face when they heard it.

Seated at a table in the Oasis Saloon, Brent held up his glass and made a toast.

"Here's to the gun slinging mayor of Gila Bend. May he live to be a hundred," Brent said.

Raymond D. Mason

"Here, here," Grant said and clicked his glass against Brent's.

The two of them laughed and took a drink. As Brent lowered his glass he glanced in the direction of the saloon doors just as the three deserters entered. Something about their demeanor told Brent they were bad news.

He eyed them warily causing Grant to notice, "What is it, Brent...uh, John T?"

The three men that just entered; they sure look like they could be the ones the cavalry patrol told us about," Brent said.

Grant casually turned and gave the three men a look also. He looked back at Brent and agreed readily, "You're right about that."

"I think I'll get a little closer and see if one of them has a German accent," Brent said.

"Be careful, we don't want to draw anymore attention to us than we already have," Grant said.

Brent grinned, "Don't worry, little brother...my name is John T. Holt, remember."

Grant chuckled lightly as Brent got up and walked to the bar where the three men were standing. Walking up next to the larger man of the three, Brent called to the bartender, "We'd like another beer when you get a chance."

The big German turned and gave Brent a hard look. Brent looked back at the man and held his gaze on him.

"Und vat are you looking at," the German said with a definite accent.

"Beats me, partner; I just wanted a beer," Brent replied.

A Distant Thunder

The German pondered Brent's response for a moment and then let it pass when he couldn't determine if it was a put down or not. The shorter man of the tree, however, had caught the meaning of the comment and spoke up.

"He said he didn't know what you were, Sarge."

Hearing the German accent and then hearing the man referred to as 'Sarge' confirmed Brent's suspicions. The last thing he wanted was to get tangled up with these three.

"Hey, I didn't mean anything by it. How about I buy you boys a beer," Brent said.

"We're drinking whiskey," the smaller man said.

"Then I'll buy you a whiskey. My friend and I were going to have one more beer and then call it a night," Brent said.

The German glared at Brent and uttered, "I don't tink I like you very much."

Brent was in no mood to take much off these three. Perhaps it was because he was still somewhat upset about his run-in with the sheriff, but it didn't take much to ruffle his feathers, so to speak.

"Look, I don't care if you like me or not. You can buy your own drinks if you feel that way about it," Brent said and then turned his attention towards the bartender.

"Hey, barkeep, bring those beers over to our table. I need some fresh air," he said as the bartender gave him a wave as acknowledgement.

The three men watched Brent walk back to the table where Grant was sitting. Grant had kept an

73

eye on them the entire time. When Brent sat down Grant stated, "They're still watching you."

"Let 'em. I'm sure they're the ones the captain told us about. I don't like deserters," Brent stated.

Still watching them Grant said, "They turned back towards the bar. I guess they're letting whatever got 'em riled drop."

"If they don't it will be too bad for them," Brent said and then looked at Grant. "I'm not in the best of moods right now."

"I can tell," Grant replied. "The bartender is heading this way with our beers."

As the bartender rounded the bar holding the two beers by the beer glass handles, the German reached out and grabbed him by the front of the shirt.

"Uh oh," Grant said. "I think we're going to have a new waiter."

This caused Brent to look in the direction of the bar. When he saw the German take the two glasses from the bartender he pulled his pistol and held it out of sight under the table.

Hauser started walking towards Brent and Grant's table sloshing the beer as he walked. By the time he'd reached them the glasses were only half filled.

"Here is your beer, girls," Hauser said.

He placed one beer in front of Grant but never took his eyes off Brent. The other two deserters began their walk towards the table at that time. Brent didn't move a muscle, just kept his eyes on Hauser.

"Here's your beer," Hauser said threw the beer in Brent's face.

"Here's your payment," Brent said when the beer hit him and he pulled the trigger on his Colt.

The bullet hit Hauser in the stomach causing the big German's eyes to widen in surprise. He took a step back and put his hand to his stomach. It was covered with blood when he removed it. That was when Younger went for his gun, but was hit in the chest by the next bullet from Brent's gun. Quincy Talbot had pulled his pistol and aimed it at Brent.

Just as Talbot pulled the trigger, however, Hauser stumbled forward into the line of fire and took the bullet in his back. He pitched forward which gave Brent an open shot at Talbot who had flipped a table over and was hiding behind it.

Brent fired three more shots into the table at the spot where he figured the man would be. Two of the bullets hit their mark. Talbot fell backwards with a bullet wound to his shoulder and one right between the eyes.

Grant sat there with his eyes wide open and holding his pistol, but he'd never fired it. He looked quickly at Brent and then turned and looked at the three dead men.

Brent stood up and moved across to where Hauser lay. He looked down at him and then moved over to Talbot and did the same thing. Both men were dead, that was for sure. He didn't have to go to Younger, however. He could tell from where he was that he was dead. His eyes were wide open and the back of his head was gone.

Raymond D. Mason

Brent looked at the onlookers and stated loudly, "Just so you know, these are the three men the cavalry patrol was searching for. They're deserters wanted for murder."

"Yeah, I heard the cavalrymen talking about it," one of the customers said.

"That hombre took on all three of them at the same time," someone else stated.

"Fastest man with a gun I've ever seen," another said.

Before long the entire saloon was hailing Brent as the fastest gun in Arizona. He wanted out of there before the law showed up, whoever that may be. He and Grant hurried out to a few pats on the back and 'atta boys'.

As soon as they arrived back at the hotel where they had put up when they hit town, Brent told Cheryl to have the kids ready to leave early the next morning. He hoped it would take the locals that long to find out where they were staying.

12

October 6, 1879
Buffalo Gap, Texas

Terrin Gibbons looked mournfully out her bedroom window. She was heartsick at the way her life was turning out. She had been so sure of her feelings for Brian until she met Dan Travers, the bank president. Now she feared she had lost both men.

Terrin had never been attracted to a man to the point of wanting to be married to him; that is until she had met Brian. He had been what she had always wanted in a man. He was strong, brave, tall and good looking; a man of good character, and a man who would take care of his woman. He had proven that.

Dan, too, was that kind of man. He wasn't as handsome as Brian, but he certainly wasn't a homely man. He had all the attributes Brian had; at least that was what she thought. Now though, it appeared she may have to live her life without either of them.

Lost in her thoughts she didn't hear the rap on the door until the second time the person knocked. Having her thoughts jarred back to the present, Terrin walked to the door and opened it. It was the sheriff of Buffalo Gap, Sheriff Bob Payne.

"Oh, hello Sheriff...I see you're back from pursuing the bank robbers. What brings you to see me?" Terrin asked curiously.

"Yes, we just got back. We caught up to them when one of their horses came up lame and they had to double up," the sheriff said and then paused. "Do you mind if I come in, Terrin? There are some things I need to ask you about and I don't want to run the risk of anyone else overhearing us," Sheriff Payne said.

"Come in, please," Terrin said as she stepped aside for him to enter.

"This might seem strange, I know, but there's been a few things brought to my attention that I need to talk to you about," the sheriff said with a slight frown.

"Go ahead, ask me anything you'd like, please," Terrin said with a confused look on her face.

"Okay, then I will. Did Dan ever say any thing to you about what his future plans were? I mean as far as what he wanted to do in the banking business," the sheriff asked.

"No," Terrin said thoughtfully. "He mentioned once or twice that he'd like to move to California eventually because of the opportunities out there. Why do you ask that?"

The sheriff took a deep breath and then stated, "We now have reason to believe that Dan may have actually set up the bank robbery. It certainly is beginning to look that way."

"I find that hard to believe, Sheriff. He was such a gentleman. Why do you think he may have had something to do with the robbery?"

"We found a note in one of the bank robber's pockets that indicated they had been in touch with the bank president. In fact, it looks like Dan may have set the whole thing up."

Terrin's eyes widened as she said, "You don't mean that? I just can't believe that Dan would set out to rob his own bank. What did the note say?"

The sheriff stated by memory, "Come to the back door when you get into town and I'll give you instructions as to when and how the robbery is to take place."

Terrin frowned slightly, "Well that could have been written by one of the bank robbers."

"It carried the initials 'D T'...Dan Travers. The writing compared to that of Dan's. We checked it out," Sheriff Payne said.

"Dan...behind the robbery," Terrin said to herself.

"He never said anything to you about needing, or wanting to make more money? Nothing that might fit in with his being involved in the robbery?" the sheriff questioned.

"No, nothing," Terrin said, "If there was I don't remember it at all."

"Okay, I guess that's all the questions I have for you. If you should think of something later on, I hope you'll let me know about it," the sheriff said as he prepared to go.

"I will...yes, of course," Terrin said, her mind in a swirl.

"I'm sorry to be the bearer of sad tidings this way, but that goes along with the job," the sheriff said politely.

Terrin nodded as she tried to sort things out in her mind. The sheriff said goodbye and left. Terrin stood there and just stared at the doorway for several long seconds before turning and walking to the window.

"Dan...how could you?" She said. And then was quiet for a moment before saying in a near whisper, "I'm so sorry Brian. Oh, what have I done? I should have known...I should have known."

October 11, 1879
The Sackett Ranch

John Sackett looked at his youngest son and cleared his throat. Brian turned from the window and looked at his pa with a frown on his face.

"I want to talk to you, Brian," John said.

"Go ahead, what is it?" Brian said in a tight voice.

"It's about the way you've been going on around here for the last couple of days. Something is eating at you and I want to know what it is. AJ said you almost took one of the ranch hand's head off this morning over next to nothing. What's eating you," John said firmly.

"It's no one's business but my own. I just, well I just...never mind, this is something I have to work out on my own," Brian snapped.

"You've made it our business by your attitude towards everyone around you. Now if you're in trouble or have a problem I want to know about it," John replied.

"Look Pa, I have to deal with something that is no one's concern but my own. When I'm ready I'll talk about it. I'm not ready now, so leave me alone" Brian said almost angrily.

John held a hard, steady gaze at his son and finally said, "Don't use that tone of voice with me; not in my house."

"Okay, then I'll get out of your house. I have to go to town anyway," Brian said and grabbed his hat as he headed for the door.

"That's another thing. You've been doing a lot of drinking lately. I suppose that has to do with your problem as well as your attitude," John stated.

Brian didn't say anything until he had opened the door. He turned back towards his father and said, "I suppose it does, Pa."

With that Brian went downstairs and out the front door. John followed after his son and by the time he reached the door, Brian was already mounting up on his horse that was tied at the hitching rail in front of the house.

John watched him ride away and slowly shook his head. Something was tearing his son up inside, but he couldn't help him if his boy wouldn't tell him what was wrong. He knew Brian well enough, or at least he had in the past, to know that when he was ready he would open up and do a soul cleansing. At least, that was John's hope.

Raymond D. Mason

12

October 11, 1879
Yuma, Arizona

Cheyanne LeFevre opened the door to the sheriff's office and peered inside. The sheriff was seated behind his desk and looked up when he heard the door open. Cheyanne looked back as though making sure no one was watching her before stepping inside.

"Can I help you, young lady?" the sheriff asked.

"I hope so, Sheriff. I am trying to find a man by the name of Clyde Johnson. I was told that he'd moved to Yuma last year. Do you happen to know if there's someone by that name living around these parts?" Cheyanne asked.

"Clyde Johnson, eh," the sheriff said with a slight grin, "And, just what is it you want to speak with Mr. Johnson about?"

Cheyanne hesitated before stating firmly, "That is between Mr. Johnson and me, Sheriff."

The sheriff chuckled slightly and then slowly got to his feet. He was a very large man, standing around 6'7" tall and weighing around 280 pounds. He smiled at Cheyanne and then said, "I'm Clyde Johnson. Maybe I should say, newly elected sheriff Clyde Johnson."

Cheyanne's eyes widened as she stared at this mountain of a man. He held his hand out towards a chair that was placed in front of his desk and said, "Have a seat and tell me what it is you'd like to talk to me about."

"Oh, Sheriff, I had no idea you were the sheriff here. I thought you were a rancher?" Cheyanne said.

"I am. I have a very capable man running my ranch and Yuma was in need of a sheriff, so I ran for the office and won in a landslide," Sheriff Johnson said. "Now what is your name and what is it you'd like to talk to me about?"

"My name is Cheyanne LeFevre," she said and paused to see if her last name meant anything to the sheriff. When he merely smiled at her she went on, "I'm here to warn you," she said.

Sheriff Johnson nodded his head and said, "About Harmon's escape from prison?"

Cheyanne looked surprised, "Yes, how'd you know?"

Johnson chuckled as he said, "The telegraph is a wonderful invention. I received a wire the day after Harmon and Kenton broke out. I must say, though, I'm a little surprised that you, his sister, would come to warn me about him."

"I'm his half sister. Harmon and I have never been really close. I certainly don't approve of his lifestyle and I didn't want to see an innocent person harmed by my brother," Cheyanne said truthfully.

"I appreciate that, young lady, I truly do. So, I take it that Harmon is headed this way, am I right?"

"Yes, him and his friend, Kenton," Cheyanne said and then went on. "I'm on my way to California, but couldn't pass through here without warning you about my brother."

"Whereabouts are you thinking of going in California?"

"I don't know...I guess maybe San Francisco. I'm a singer," Cheyanne said.

"Oh, a singer," the sheriff said. "Well, if I ever get out to San Francisco I'll be sure and look you up."

Cheyanne smiled as she stood up. Sheriff Johnson, who had sat back down, also got to his feet. He moved around the desk and towards the door as Cheyanne started that way.

Turning to face the sheriff, Cheyanne said, "I hope you don't have to hurt Harmon, Sheriff. I just want to see him go back to prison."

"We'll try our best to take him alive; I can assure you of that. Do you know if they are coming by train or by horseback?" the sheriff asked.

"They were planning on coming by train, but they may get off somewhere and come in by stagecoach or on horseback," Cheyanne said.

"I'd say they'll definitely come by horseback now. That is, if Harmon knows you were going to warn me."

Raymond D. Mason

"He may figure it out. He's always thought he was smarter than me, but he never fooled me once; not even when we were kids," Cheyanne said peering up at the massive man in front of her.

"Well, good luck on your trip to California. And don't worry your pretty little head; we'll do our best to take your brother alive," Sheriff Johnson said.

Cheyanne smiled thankfully and walked outside onto the boardwalk. She looked up and down the street while the sheriff watched her. When he saw she was unsure of her surroundings he offered his advice.

"If you're looking for a place to stay until the next train leaves, the hotel right down the street there is a good place to stay," the sheriff said pointing in the direction of the hotel.

"I'm a little hungry. Where do you recommend eating at?"

"The hotel has a fine restaurant and they're not over priced like a lot of hotel restaurants are," Sheriff Johnson said.

"Thank you, Sheriff," Cheyanne said as she carried her one carpetbag and headed towards the hotel.

Sheriff Johnson watched her walk away and then went back inside his office. He walked over to the gun rack and took a Henry repeating rifle out and carried it to his desk.

The sheriff opened the desk drawer and took out a box of cartridges and started loading the long, shiny barreled rifle. He would try to take Harmon

LeFevre alive, but if he couldn't he'd have to take him down...hard.

Cheyanne walked up to the registry desk in the hotel lobby and set her valise down. She looked around for the clerk, but couldn't spot anyone. Seeing the small bell on the counter she picked it up and gave it a ring. A man appeared quickly through a curtain in back of the desk and smiled warmly.

"I'm sorry I was just having my meal. I take it you would like a room?" he asked, turning the hotel registry around where Cheyanne could sign it.

"Yes, do you have one with a bath?" Cheyanne asked.

"There is a room for bathing on each floor," he said proudly. "Just let us know about a half hour before you want to bathe and we'll have the bath ready for you."

"Okay, I'd like one in about a half hour," Cheyanne said as she signed the registry.

"Certainly, madam, here is your key. Room 203 at the head of the stairs; it will be the second door on your right," the clerk said as he pointed up the stairs.

"Thank you," Cheyanne said.

"How long will you be staying with us?"

"Until the next train to California, I guess."

"Oh, I see. That would be tomorrow at 3:05 in the afternoon," the clerk said helpfully.

Cheyanne went up the stairs to room 203. She unlocked the door and went in, placing her valise on the bed and taking out the clothes she would be changing into.

She laid out a men's black shirt and a pair of men's black pants. She also removed a pair of black boots with a riding heel and then a black Stetson hat. The last thing she removed was a black gun belt and holster with a pearl handled Colt .45 in it.

Cheyanne then went to the small table and picked up a towel and tossed it onto the bed next to the other things. She looked in the long mirror next to the door and grinned slightly as she slowly began to take her clothes off in preparation for her bath.

"You'll need some traveling money if you're going to San Francisco," Cheyanne said to herself. "And I saw a nice little bank that will give you exactly what you need."

13

After taking her bath Cheyanne went back to her room and got dressed in the clothes she'd laid out. Once she had dressed she reached in the pants back pocket and pulled out a black mask that would cover her entire face except for the slits cut in the mask so she could see. It was now nearing 4:00 pm.

Cheyanne pushed the mask back into the pocket and put the Stetson on, pushing her hair up under it. She walked to the door and opened it just enough so she could look out into the hallway. Assured there was no one around, Cheyanne hurried down the hall to a door that led to an outside staircase.

The Cattlemen's Association Bank of Yuma was just down the street from where the hotel was located. Cheyanne went down the stairs and then across the narrow alleyway. She made sure there was no one in the alley and then took another alleyway that led along the back of the various businesses.

When Cheyanne reached the back door of the bank, she tried it and found that it was locked. Not wanting to go around to the front door where she might be spotted, she waited behind a water barrel at the side of the bank where she slipped the black mask on over her head.

After about four or five minutes the back door opened and a man stepped outside carrying a wastepaper basket. The man was one of the bank clerks. The clerk didn't see Cheyanne and as he turned to go back inside she made her move. She rushed up behind the man and stuck the barrel of the pistol in to his back.

"Just do as you're told and you won't get hurt," Cheyanne said in her deepest voice, and with a slight accent.

The clerk slowly raised his hands and they both entered the bank through the back door. There were only two other people in the bank; another bank clerk and the bank's president.

No one noticed Cheyanne following the man, until the bank president looked in his direction and saw him standing with his hands raised.

"What are you doing there...," the president started to say and then stopped short.

"This guy was waiting for me outside," the bank clerk said.

With that the other bank clerk turned and looked to see what the two were talking about. As soon as he saw what was going on he started to make a break for the front door.

"One more step and this man is dead," Cheyanne yelled out.

"Stop Higgins...do you want to get me killed," the man Cheyanne was holding her gun on yelled out.

The teller stopped and slowly raised his hands. The bank president looked towards the teller's window where they kept a pistol under the countertop and had the urge to go for it.

Cheyanne motioned for the man who had started to make a break for it to move back into the middle of the bank. She cast a quick glance at the bank president and noticed his eyes peering towards the teller's side of the teller's window.

Without a word she moved over to the window and picked up the pistol hidden there. She looked at the president and shook her head slightly as she said, "Ah, ah, ah."

"What do you want?" the president asked.

"Now what do you think? I want two thousand dollars," Cheyanne said calmly.

One of the bank clerks cast a curious glance at Cheyanne and then at the other teller. He took a close look at the size of the bank robber and the depth of the voice. He grinned slightly as he figured out that they were being robbed by a woman.

"Two thousand dollars?" the banker questioned.

"That's right. I don't want any more than that. Now get it and no one will get hurt," Cheyanne said.

"Two thousand?" the banker repeated.

"Yes...now quit stalling and get the money."

The banker went to the safe and began dialing the lock's combination. He was totally perplexed at the bank robber's demand for only two thousand dollars. Why not five, or ten thousand? The bank certainly had it.

As the bank president thought of the situation a small grin pulled at the corners of his mouth. He knew for a fact that the bank had over twenty five thousand dollars in cash in the safe. He should, he'd just put it there.

Cheyanne had the other two men move over by the banker so she could keep an eye on all of them at the same time. Her eyes darted from one man to another.

The banker dialed the last number and turned the safe's handle. The door swung lazily open which caused Cheyanne to move closer. Satisfied there wasn't another pistol in the safe, she moved back slightly.

The banker pulled four stacks of bills out that totaled exactly two thousand dollars; five hundred dollars in each stack. He handed the bills to Cheyanne who took them and then backed towards the back door of the bank.

"If any of you poke your head out that back door, I'll put a bullet in your head. Have you got that?" she said tightly.

They all three nodded their answers. Cheyanne slowly opened the door and peeked out. There was no one in the alley so after shoving the money into her shirt, she stepped outside.

Cheyanne made a mad dash down the alleyway to and around the corner. She bounded up the outside stairs of the hotel and quickly stepped into the hotel hallway. She ran on tiptoes down the hall to her room and unlocked the door and slipped inside.

Meanwhile back at the bank something out of the ordinary was taking place. One of the bank tellers said excitedly, "That was a woman that robbed us."

"I know it. I could tell by the sound of her voice and the faint smell of perfume she was wearing," the banker said.

"I'll go for the sheriff," the other teller said.

"Hold on, Virgil. Let's not rush this too much," the president said causing the other two to give him a curious look.

"What is it, Mr. Dickerson?" one of the men asked.

"I want us to be clear on something. I have been aware that a few dollars here and there have been missing at the end of the work day. Now I didn't say anything because I wanted the guilty party to come to me and tell me what they had been doing," the president stated.

"It wasn't me," one of the men said quickly.

"Hey, it wasn't me either," the other man said.

"I don't care who it was, but I know it was one of you. Now listen up. That 'woman' only took $2,000. We have around $35,000 left in this safe," the president started.

Both men nodded in agreement as the president continued, "Now I don't know about you

Raymond D. Mason

men, but I could definitely use $10,000...couldn't you?"

The two men frowned slightly until it dawned on them what the president was getting at. They cast quick glances at one another and then zeroed in on the president.

"So what are you saying?"

"We split what's left in the safe and tell the sheriff the bandit got away with $32,000. Who is to know, but us?"

"The woman who robbed us will know," one of the tellers said.

"Yes, but she'll tell *only* if she gets caught," the banker grinned. "If we tell the sheriff it was a man who stood around six feet tall the sheriff wouldn't even be looking for the woman."

The two men thought over what the president was offering and after considering the proposal out nodded slowly in agreement.

"I could sure use some extra money...what with the baby coming this spring," one of the men said.

"And my wife has been sickly and under a doctor's care. Who knows what that might lead to," the other man agreed.

"It's settled then. We'll each take $10,000. Let's go over the story we're going to tell the sheriff so we don't get the details mixed up," the president said.

The men all looked at one another and began to smile. As the president began to count out each man's share the smiles got bigger. The president held the biggest smile of all. He had been dipping into the banks funds and this would cover it up.

A Distant Thunder

Once Cheyanne was inside her hotel room she quickly got out of the men's clothes she had donned and packed them into the valise. She hid the money in a side pocket of the valise and then slipped into a dressing gown and sat down on the edge of the bed.

She let out a long sigh of relief and smiled demurely as she thought of what she had just done. She took a deep breath and then got up and walked over to a where her handbag was sitting on a small table in the room.

She took a small note pad out of her purse along with a pencil. She sat down at the table and scribbled out a note and tore the sheet of paper off the pad. Cheyanne checked what she had written. She then stuck the note in her skirt pocket and walked back to the bed and sat down on it again. She let out a big sigh of relief as she closed her eyes and fell straight back onto the bed.

Cheyanne was exhausted due to the extraordinary amount of adrenaline she had burned from the excitement of robbing another bank. Unbeknownst to her half-brother Harmon, Cheyanne had turned to robbing banks when she needed money, but always in small amounts and also to reveal crooked bankers in the process.

Not once in the three other bank robberies she'd pulled had the men involved ever told the authorities that they had been robbed by a woman. She knew it wasn't that she had been able to convince them that she was a man, but rather to lead the authorities away from that fact.

Meanwhile the bank president had run out onto the street and began yelling, "Robbed...the bank's been robbed!"

Very quickly the word about the robbery reached Sheriff Johnson and he hurried to the bank where he met with three very upset men. They were shaking like leaves on a tree. In fact, the sheriff thought they were a little too upset.

"So tell me what happened," the sheriff said.

"I went out back to take the trash out to the barrel for burning and the man dressed all in black stuck a gun in my back and told me he'd kill me if I didn't do exactly as he said," the teller who Cheyanne had first confronted said.

"The man was dressed all in black?" the sheriff repeated.

"Yes, he was...and he was a big man. I'd say he was close to you in size, Sheriff," the bank president added.

"Okay, go on," Sheriff Johnson said looking from one man to the next.

"Well, he shoved me inside the bank and yelled to the others to put up their hands," the man went on.

The bank president took over the conversation then, "Yes, that's right and he cocked the hammer back on his pistol and held it to my head and made me unlock the safe. He said if I didn't do it he would blow my head off."

"What did you two do while he was doing this?" the sheriff asked.

"Oh, he'd made us lie down on the floor," one of the men said quickly.

"Face down," the president added.

"How much money did the robber get?" Sheriff Johnson questioned.

"Over thirty thousand dollars," the president replied.

"You already know that for sure?" Clyde asked thoughtfully.

"We'd just counted it out and put it in the safe; that's how I know exactly how much was taken," the president answered.

"Then what did he do?" the sheriff asked.

"Well...he went out the back door and told us that he had a man out front who would shoot us if we went out within ten minutes of the time he left. We weren't about to take a chance," the president said looking at the other two men.

"Once the ten minutes were up, I looked out and when I didn't see anyone I ran out and announced that we'd been robbed," the president said, getting agreeing nods from the other two men.

"You didn't see which way the man headed when he left here?"

"No, Sheriff...we were too scared to look out the back door," the banker stated.

"Okay, I'll have to see if anyone else saw anything suspicious. First, however, I'll see if I can find any horseshoe tracks to indicate which way he headed when he left here," Sheriff Johnson said as he moved towards the back door.

Raymond D. Mason

"We didn't hear any hoof beats, Sheriff. We figured he must have had his horse tied somewhere else," the president said quickly.

Sheriff Johnson walked outside and checked the ground for anything that might help him in his investigation of the robbery. What he saw on the ground outside bothered him greatly.

For one thing there were boot tracks that indicated the bank robber had waited behind a rain barrel. He could easily see where the robber had moved up behind the teller who had came out to dump the trash.

As he looked at the footprints he spotted the direction the robber had both come and gone. He'd gone from the bank in the same direction he'd approached it. That was easy enough to see; but, something about the tracks bothered the sheriff.

The president had described the bank robber as a big man; close to him in size. The footprints he was looking at didn't seem to match up. These footprints indicated a much smaller man had made them. In fact, the bank robber's boot size was smaller than the teller who had first been confronted by the robber.

Something didn't seem quite right about this holdup. It would do no good to round up a posse, seeing as how there was no trail to follow. All he could do was begin asking people around town if they'd seen a very large man dressed in black. Naturally he would investigate the robbery, but something's just didn't add up.

14

12:05 am
October 12, 1879

Cheyanne LaFevre sat at the window of her hotel room and watched the sheriff's office. She'd learned that the sheriff always made his rounds around midnight and was waiting for him to start them before doing what she had to do next.

At 12:10 am, Sheriff Johnson walked out onto the boardwalk in front of his office carrying a sawed off shotgun. He looked up and down the street and then headed off to his right.

Cheyanne wasted no time in making her move. She hurried to the back stairs again and down to the street level. Making sure no one saw her she crossed the street so she was on the same side as the sheriff's office.

Staying against the buildings she made her way to the sheriff's office undetected. When she reached the office and jail she opened the door and peeked inside. No one was there, so she slipped inside and went to the sheriff's desk.

She pulled the note she had written out earlier and placed in the middle of his desk so he couldn't miss it. She hurried back to the door and peeked out again to see if anyone was nearby. The only ones around were a couple of men on horseback who were riding by on their way towards the saloon near the hotel where she was staying.

Cheyanne went back to the hotel and up to her room sure that no one had seen her near the sheriff's office. She picked up her valise and walked down the hall to the stairs that led to the front lobby.

The night clerk was on duty and when he saw her smiled warmly, "Are you going out so late at night?" he asked.

"No, I'm going to the train station to catch the late night train to the City of Angels...Los Angeles," she replied.

"Oh, you're leaving us. Well, I hope you enjoyed your stay here," the clerk said.

"I did, thank you. Do I owe you anything?" she asked.

"No, you covered it when you checked in," the man said.

"Goodbye," she said and walked to the front door.

"Goodnight and please come back again," the man said in return.

"Oh, I will do that," Cheyanne said and exited the hotel.

Cheyanne left the hotel and went directly to the train depot. She had checked the schedule earlier and learned there was a train coming in that was bound for Los Angeles. She wanted to be onboard that train when if pulled out. What she didn't know was that Harmon LaFevre and Jeb Kenton would be on that train coming in from the east.

Sheriff Clyde Johnson walked along the main street of Yuma checking the doors of the various businesses to make sure they were locked. He held the shotgun in one hand as he made his way up one side of the street and then down the other.

The sheriff looked in on every saloon in town during his rounds and usually found them free of any real trouble. He might have to break up an occasional fist fight, but hardly ever anything worse than that.

Upon finishing his rounds the sheriff returned to his office to wait for the deputy that would come in at 2 am to relieve him. He unloaded the shotgun before placing it back in the rack and then went to his desk to sit down.

Noticing the handwritten note on his desk he frowned slightly as he picked it up and read what it said. It was the note Cheyanne had left there and read as follows:

> ***Sheriff,***
> ***I robbed the bank here in Yuma today and took $2,000; no more, no less. I wanted you to know the exact amount I stole because I doubt that is what the banker will report as being taken. I am under 5' 8" tall and my weight is well below 150 pounds.***

Sheriff Johnson read the note and a grin slowly spread across his face. He'd thought that something didn't fit with what he'd observed when investigating the robbery and this confirmed it. It looked like there had been two robberies at the bank.

The first robbery was committed by a small bank robber who stole $2,000 and the second robbery was committed by the banker and the two tellers for something like $30,000. This wasn't the first time something like this had happened and he doubted it would be the last.

The sheriff looked at the clock on the office wall and saw that it was nearing 2 am. He knew there was a train due in from the east and he'd been meeting every train since he'd heard that Harmon LeFevre had escaped to see if Harmon was one of the passengers getting off.

Just then the deputy showed up to relieve Sheriff Johnson and the sheriff headed for the train depot before going home. When he got there the first person he saw was Cheyanne LeFevre. She was sitting inside with her valise next to her.

When Cheyanne saw the sheriff she smiled and nodded as he approached where she was seated. When he stopped in front of her she looked up at him and said, "I'm on my way to California."

"Yes, I can see that. You sure took a late train. You know that there'll be one around three o'clock this afternoon, don't you?" the sheriff asked.

Cheyanne smiled and chuckled slightly, "Yes, but the rowdies outside the hotel room where I was trying to sleep convinced me to take this train."

"Yeah, they can do that. You should be here on a Saturday night if you want rowdies," the sheriff grinned.

"I don't want rowdies, thank you. I'm anxious to get to California. I've heard so much about it. Of course, like I told you before, I'll be going on up to San Francisco," Cheyanne stated firmly.

"Yes, I remember you saying that," the sheriff said and then asked. "Did you hear about the bank being robbed today?"

"I heard someone say it had been, yes. Did you catch the man who robbed it?" Cheyanne said.

"Man?" the sheriff said.

"Yes...I heard it was one man. A large man from what the hotel clerk told me."

The sheriff eyed her suspiciously, but didn't press the conversation. He did, however, glance down at the valise and the thought crossed his mind as to whether or not he might find some black clothes inside.

Raymond D. Mason

15

Cheyanne watched the sheriff closely and then looked towards the loading platform. She saw the stationmaster waving his red lantern so the train engineer would know where to stop for the un-boarding of the passengers.

"Oh, it looks like my train is coming in," Cheyanne said.

Sheriff Johnson looked out and saw the train pulling in. He looked down at Cheyanne and then at the grip.

"Here, let me help you with that," the sheriff said as he bent down and picked up the carpetbag.

Cheyanne tensed slightly, but didn't let it show. The sheriff moved up to where the passenger cars would be stopping and waited as the engine pulled passed on its way to where the stationmaster was standing.

The train only had three passenger cars and Sheriff Johnson was standing where the first car would be stopping. Cheyanne stood by the sheriff and when the train jerked to a halt took the carpetbag from him.

"Thank you, Sheriff; I can handle it from here," she said.

"I hope you'll come back to Yuma one day?" Sheriff Johnson said.

"I just may do that. I hope everything works out okay should Harmon ever show up here. I just pray you don't have to harm him, but he really should be in prison," Cheyanne stated.

"I hope so too. And, thank you for letting me know about him. That was very big of you," the sheriff smiled.

The conductor stepped off the train and held the door open for the lone passenger for that car. A few other people were waiting for the passengers who were disembarking from those cars.

As Cheyanne stepped into the first passenger car two men were stepping out of the third car onto the platform. It was Harmon LaFevre and Jeb Kenton. They casually looked around and when they turned and looked in the direction of Sheriff Johnson, LaFevre froze.

Sheriff Johnson tipped his hat towards Cheyanne and glanced to his left. At first he didn't even recognize Harmon LeFevre, but when he saw the man suddenly go for his gun, reacted quickly.

"It's him," LeFevre yelled out.

Jeb Kenton instantly went for his gun also, although not as quickly as LeFevre had made his draw. Harmon's gun roared first, the bullet hitting the sheriff in the left shoulder. The second gunshot that sounded came from the sheriff's gun and its bullet hit LeFevre in the right side, spinning him around.

A Distant Thunder

Kenton's shot missed the sheriff, but hit the conductor who had stepped off the train to hold the door open. Kenton broke towards a loading cart on the platform, but the sheriff's second shot hit him in the left hip and knocked him to the ground.

Kenton fired another shot from his prone position and the bullet hit the sheriff in his gun hand. The force of the bullet knocked the gun out of the sheriff's hand and sent it skidding down the platform.

LaFevre had managed to get to his feet after having dropped to one knee and when he saw the sheriff was now unarmed, began moving slowly towards him.

Kenton's hip was injured to a point he could not even get to his feet and as he lay there watching what was taking place between LaFevre and the sheriff failed to notice the stationmaster moving up behind him with a pistol aimed at him.

Kenton started to raise his pistol and shoot at the now unarmed sheriff when the stationmaster said tightly, "Don't even think about it. Now drop the gun or I'll blow your head clean off your shoulders."

Kenton instantly dropped his pistol and the stationmaster kicked it away from him before looking at what was happening further down the tracks. He couldn't fire at Harmon because the sheriff was between him and LaFevre.

Holding his side, LaFevre walked laboriously towards the sheriff with his pistol raised and aimed at the unarmed sheriff. A tight smile managed to

107

momentarily crack through the pain of the wound to his side, grotesquely contorting his face.

"I've been waiting a long time to do this, Johnson. Now you're going to pay for what you put me through," LaFevre said through clenched teeth. "Adios."

Suddenly a shot rang out, but it was not from Harmon's gun, it came from someone in the train's passenger car. The bullet hit Harmon in the right shoulder, but from the side. The bullet passed through his shoulder.

Although the bullet had done severe damage to Harmon's heart he didn't die instantly. The force of the bullet spun him to the side so he was facing in the direction from which the bullet had come.

The bullet had come through the opened window of the passenger car even with where Harmon was standing. He saw face on the person who had shot him. It was Cheyanne LaFevre, Harmon's half sister.

Harmon slowly held one hand out in Cheyanne's direction while his face held the question, 'why'? Cheyanne slowly lowered the gun in her hand as a tear slowly trickled down her cheek.

Harmon LaFevre crumpled to the platform and died. Sheriff Johnson walked slowly up to where Harmon's body lay and looked down at him. He slowly turned and looked through the passenger's window of the train and saw Cheyanne standing there; the gun now hanging at her side.

Several onlookers began to assemble around the sheriff and Harmon's dead body. The stationmaster had sent a young man to bring the doctor and the deputy that Sheriff Johnson has left on duty.

Cheyanne walked off the train and up alongside the sheriff. She had a stunned look on her face as she peered down at Harmon's still body.

"I couldn't let him shoot you," she said quietly.

The sheriff nodded his head knowingly, "Thank you, Miss. I know that had to be one of the hardest things you ever had to do."

"I suppose you'll want me to stay here while there is a court hearing?" Cheyanne asked.

The sheriff thought about if for a moment and then shook his head negatively, "I don't see why you should have to remain around here. It's pretty obvious what happened and there were plenty of witnesses."

Cheyanne slowly looked up into the sheriff's face and asked, "You don't have any other questions you want to ask me?"

"No, I don't. I'd say you have answered all the questions I might ask of you. In fact, I may even have your testimony in writing and in my top desk drawer," the sheriff said, referring to the note she'd left on his desk.

Cheyanne knew what he meant and looked somewhat shocked. She figured the note and the shooting of her brother would force the sheriff to question her in regards to the bank robbery. It appeared to her that he wasn't even considering questioning her about the robbery.

After another five minutes the loading platform was cleared of dead and wounded except for the

Raymond D. Mason

sheriff. Right on schedule the conductor called out, "All aboard!"

The sheriff looked at Cheyanne and smiled, "Have a nice trip."

"Thank you, Sheriff. And I hope you have a wonderful life," Cheyanne said as the train jerked to a slow rolling start on the remainder of its journey to Los Angeles.

Cheyanne watched the sheriff for as long as she could and then took a seat next to the window. He had let her go suspecting she was the one who'd robbed the bank. She thought it had to be because she had saved his life; but was it?

Sheriff Johnson stood and watched the train build up speed as it moved on down the tracks. There was no doubt in the sheriff's mind that Cheyanne had been the lone bank robber the president and tellers had told him about.

The sheriff knew how difficult it had to have been for the young lady to shoot and kill her brother. He also felt that since she had more than likely been the one who left the note on his desk, that she was not the bank robber the president and his tellers were. She'd gotten $2,000 while they had each made off with possibly five times that amount.

He'd be having a long talk with the president and his tellers, but it would have to wait until morning. Right then he wanted nothing more than to get to the doctor and have his hand looked after and then get some much needed sleep.

The sheriff gave one last look in the direction of the train as it slowly disappeared into the darkness. He hoped Miss LeFevre found what she was looking for in California...he truly did.

Raymond D. Mason

16

**5:45 am
October 12, 1879
Gila Bend, Arizona**

Brent and the others traveling with him gave the town of Gila Bend one last look as they rode out on their journey west. Brent was glad to be on the move again. As long as he was moving he felt the law wouldn't catch up to him.

Cheryl Keeling looked over at him as he rode alongside the wagon on his horse and thought to herself, "Brent is quite a handsome man. He's somewhat hard to figure out, but deep down I think he's a good man."

It wasn't so much that Mrs. Keeling was falling in love with Brent as it was that she wished the best for him. He had helped her and the others so much with their struggles even while having to deal with his own.

She'd be glad to get to California where she might begin to truly live again. The loss of her husband was waning more everyday. That's not to

Raymond D. Mason

say that she didn't still miss him, she did, but time was doing its work of healing her wounds.

Grant Holt still missed his wife Grace and every time he peered into the face of little Gracie felt he could see a bit more of her mother reflected in the little girl. He was now beginning to wonder if he would ever find a woman who could match what he had loved so much about his late wife.

The Thurston kids wondered what might happen to them in the future. They had lost both their real parents and their foster parents and were merely 'along for the ride', so to speak. They felt safe in the company of Brent, but what if something happened to him? What would become of them?

Everyone seemed to be lost in their thoughts, but when Annie Thurston began to sing a children's song they all snapped out of their thoughts at the same time. Brent looked towards the wagon and grinned. He'd become attached to the Thurston kids, something he knew would have pleased his Julia immensely.

The trip to Yuma would be a difficult one. There was always the chance of running into some hostile Indians and these parts were known for outlaw gangs. Still, it was good to be on the move again.

Brent called out to Cheryl and Grant that he was going to ride on ahead and check the trail. They waved as he rode off; both hoping nothing happened to him like it had before when his horse had thrown him and he'd lost his memory for some time.

Brent still suffered a slight headache from time to time, mainly due to the heat than to the concussion he'd received earlier. He would be glad to get to Yuma because the trip to California would be nearing its end. Where they would go once they reached California was still up in the air. They had plenty of time to decide that, however.

Brent had ridden about a mile when he topped a rise. What he saw about a mile or so ahead brought a smile to his face. Three wagons were making their way in the direction of Yuma. He hoped the people wouldn't mind taking on another wagon as he kicked his horse into an easy lope.

He caught the three covered wagons in short order and as he rode up a man on horseback rode back to meet him. The man held up his hand in a friendly wave as they approached one another.

"Howdy, friend," the man said. "Where are you headed?"

"Hello, my family and I are headed out to California. Our wagon is a couple of miles back behind there," Brent said pointing behind him. "I was wondering if you would mind if we joined up with you. I take it you're headed for Yuma?"

"That we are and we'd be more than pleased to have you join up with us. The more there are, the safer the travel, that's what I've always said," the man said.

"Where were you planning on making camp?" Brent asked.

"We were told there was a good spot about a days travel from Gila Bend. We figured on staying the night there," the man replied.

115

"That sounds good to me. We'll catch up when you make camp," Brent said with a grin.

"My name is Mike McManus. What's yours?"

Brent caught himself just in time and answered, "The name is John T. Holt. I'll introduce the rest of my family tonight when we catch up with you."

"We'll do that, John," Mr. McManus said.

Brent reined his horse around and headed back to tell the others about their good fortune. He knew that Cheryl would be thankful to have women folks around to talk to and the kids would be excited to having other kids to run and play with. He and Grant would be thankful for the extra firepower should the need arise.

"Oh, that is good news, John T. Holt," Cheryl said with a smile and looked quickly at Grant.

"Okay, okay," Grant laughed. "You remembered to call Br...John T. by his name. Don't worry about me, young lady; I'll be all right."

"I hope so. The man I talked to seemed like good people. If the rest of them are anything like him we'll be very welcome," Brent stated.

"I hope it's not too late when we catch up to them," Cheryl said thoughtfully. "I'd like to meet the women tonight rather than having to wait till morning when we'll all be busy getting ready to pull out again."

"They're only a couple of miles ahead of us and traveling at the same rate of speed we are. If we keep a steady pace we should catch them before dark with no trouble," Brent said.

A Distant Thunder

"It will be so good to be around women folks for a spell," Cheryl said.

"Hey, you're making us feel like we ain't good company," Grant said with a grin.

"I didn't mean it like that," Cheryl said. "I just need to talk to women about...well, about...women things."

"Don't even go there, Grant," Brent laughed. "They speak a language you and I will never know."

There was about an hour's sunlight left when Brent's wagon caught up to the McManus family at the campsite. There was a small creek that still had water in it, so they didn't have to use any of their water from their barrels for the horses, cooking or washing up.

Everyone was friendly towards the new arrivals and seemed truly thankful to have them join up with them. As one of the women put it when talking with Cheryl Keeling, 'You folks must be an answer to prayer.'

Cheryl was somewhat puzzled by the remark, but didn't pursue it any further. Later, however, she would learn that the woman had been praying for someone who could handle a gun better than the men in the party.

The McManus family and the others traveling with them were Quakers; or as they preferred to be called, 'Friends'. They were good people who practiced what they preached.

Brent noticed right away how they used 'thee' and 'thou' for those closest to them, but 'you' and

Raymond D. Mason

'your' to them. When he, Cheryl and Grant were alone he asked Cheryl if she had noticed.

"They call loved ones by thee and thou; strangers are referred to as you or yours," Cheryl explained.

"Why's that?" Brent questioned.

"It's just part of their religion, I guess," Cheryl replied.

"Oh...sounds like a lot of work to me; figuring out who you want to call 'thee' and who you want to call 'you'," Brent stated.

"I guess if you're raised that way it's a lot easier to adjust to," Cheryl said and then added. "Mrs. McManus said we were an answer to prayer, because she'd prayed that they'd find someone who could handle a gun better than their men folk. Did you hear anything like that?"

"No," Brent said and then grinned, "But I guess if you're too far away to know whether the person shooting at you is a 'thee' or 'you' they might be a little hesitant to take dead aim."

"You're terrible, Brent," Cheryl laughed.

"Aha, you said Brent," Grant exclaimed pointing an accusing finger at Cheryl. "I won, I won," he said holding his hands over his head in victory.

They all had a good laugh. They felt good about traveling with a group of people they felt they could truly trust. The trip to Yuma would be somewhat easier traveling together like this. And definitely would be safer.

17

October 13, 1879
Craig Jolly's Ranch
Tucson, Arizona

Linc Sackett and Clay Butler had been making some serious money with their bucking horse. No one had been able to stay on the horse for the ten seconds it took to win the money. They had made over a hundred dollars since arriving in Tucson.

One of the cowboys who had tried his skill at riding the horse said it was as good as a horse they had on the ranch where he worked. He said the horse had thrown every rider who tried to ride it, as well.

Linc and Clay felt the opportunity to add to their traveling rodeo was too good to pass up. They had ridden out to check out the bucking horse and it turned out to be everything the cowboy had said it was; a great buck jumper.

"How much do you want for that horse?" Linc asked the ranch owner.

"You don't mean you want to buy it, do you?" the rancher replied.

"Yeah, that's what I mean. I'll give you thirty dollars for it right now; cash money," Linc said.

"Thirty dollars for a horse no one has been able to ride? Makes no sense to me," the rancher said thoughtfully. After a few moments he said, "You wouldn't go fifty would you?"

Linc shook his head negatively, "No...but, I'll tell you what I'll do. If you throw in the halter and rope we'll give you forty dollars, how's that?"

"You just bought yourselves a horse," the rancher said and they shook hands to seal the deal.

"Pay the man, Clay," Linc said as he looked towards the animal they had just purchased.

Just as Clay was in the process of counting out the money for the horse, two riders turned off the main road and headed down the long drive to the ranch house. The rancher, Craig Jolly, saw the two men and took on a serious frown.

When Clay noticed the look on the rancher's face, he followed the gaze of Jolly and saw the two men who were approaching.

"What do those two want?" Jolly said under his breath.

"I take it you know them?" Clay said.

"I wish I didn't, but yes, I know them all right," Jolly said.

"Who are they?" Clay asked.

"That's Hutch and Wayne Wrango. I thought they would be long gone from these parts after the shooting of Bob Bell," Jolly said as the two men neared the corral area.

A Distant Thunder

"I guess they don't fear the law in these parts," Linc said having picked up on the conversation.

"They'd better fear retribution. I heard from one of my riders that he thought he saw Bill Bell heading for Tucson this morning. I'd hate to be in the Wrango brother's boots," Jolly stated.

The Wrango's rode up and looked down at Jolly, both wearing deep set frowns. Hutch Wrango spoke first.

"Jolly, we found half a dozen of our steers mingled in with your herd this morning. Have your men been moving our cattle over to your range land?" Hutch said in a near angry voice.

"Now you know better than that, Hutch. Why would I want those sorry steers of yours? I've got more cattle now than I can keep fat," Jolly replied.

"Well, just don't start trying to fatten up our cattle to take to market unless you want trouble," Hutch said.

While he was berating Jolly, Wayne Wrango was eyeing Linc and Clay. He held a disdainful glare on them which was beginning to get on both men's nerves. Finally Clay had had enough.

"What are you looking at?" he asked tightly.

"You," Wayne replied. "Don't I know you from somewhere, slick?"

"It could be, but the name ain't 'slick', slick," Clay replied with his own frown.

Jolly spoke up before the situation got too tense, "I see that Bill Bell is back in Tucson and I hear he's not too happy about the shooting of his brother Bob."

"We didn't have nothing to do with that," Hutch said quickly.

"That's not what witnesses said," Jolly answered.

"They're wrong. We weren't even in Tucson that day and we've got ten men who will vouch for us," Hutch replied.

"Ten men, huh...and they all work for your pa," Jolly said with a wry grin.

"So what if they do? Ten men are ten men; don't matter who they work for," Wayne cut in.

"Hey, you can explain that to Bill Bell when he comes looking for you two. I'm sure he'll be impressed with the testimony of wranglers on your pa's ranch," Jolly smiled.

The two brothers cast quick looks at one another and then back at Jolly.

"Just remember what we said about our cattle, Jolly. We'd better not have to come back over here again," Hutch snapped.

As they started to ride away Clay called out to Wayne, "Have you been to Cottonwood, lately?"

Wayne looked back at him and said with a scowl, "No...why would I want to go to that one horse town?"

Clay grinned, "Beats me...slick."

Wayne glared hard at Clay for several tortured seconds and then the two brothers kicked their horses up and rode back towards the main road.

"You like to live dangerously, don't you Clay?" Linc said with a laugh as they watched the two Wrango brothers ride away.

"I'd like to finish what was started in Cottonwood," Clay said getting a look from Linc.

"What actually happened up there?" Linc asked.

"I'll tell you about it someday. Right now we've got another horse to get back into Tucson," Clay said with a nod towards their newly acquired buck jumper.

Linc grinned as he eyed the horse, "Man, we could wind up millionaires if we keep going at this rate."

Clay rolled his eyes, "Dream on partner...dream on.

"So what are you boys going to do with that good for nothing Cayuse," Craig Jolly asked.

"Make a fortune Mr. Jolly...make a fortune," Linc replied.

"Come on Diamond Jim Brady," Clay said in an effort to take possession of the horse and head back to Tucson.

"Well, good luck boys," Mr. Jolly said as the two men mounted up.

"Thanks, Mr. Jolly. We'll be seeing you around, I'm sure," Linc said with a tip of his hat.

Linc rode his horse over to the gate and took the lead rope from the wrangler that was holding it. The horse followed along as gentle as a kitten. It was hard to believe this was the same horse that no one had been able to ride.

Tucson, Arizona

Raymond D. Mason

Bill Bell stood solemnly at the gravesite of his brother holding his hat in his hands and his head bowed. His eyes were closed as he thought back on their younger days; days that had been hard, but good years.

After a good five minutes Bill looked up with a somber look on his face. He put his hat on and seeing a wild flower nearby, picked it up and placed it on his brother's grave.

"I'll be back, Bob. I've got some unfinished business to take care of, but I'll be back to say a proper goodbye," Bill said quietly.

Slowly he turned and strode down the hillside to where his horse was tied. His sister in law had remained in the small farm house she and Bob had shared together since their marriage five years earlier. She was fixing some breakfast for Bill.

He rode down the hill to the house and tied up at the small hitching rail in front. Stepping down off his horse he cast another quick glance back in the direction of the family cemetery that now had two graves in it. The other was the grave of Bob and Louise's still born baby boy.

Bill walked into the house and removed his hat as he entered. He took a deep breath as he put his hat on the hat rack next to the door and next to Bob's hat. He looked at his brother's hat and grinned as he remembered how Bob always wore his hat cocked to one side.

"Breakfast is ready Bill," Louise Bell said as Bill entered the kitchen area of the house.

"I don't know how long I'll be here, Louise, but I can assure you of one thing. I'll find the ones responsible for Bob's death," Bill said.

"Or get yourself killed trying, isn't that right, Bill?" Louise said solemnly.

"Don't think like that. I've heard that the Wrango brothers were the ones who gunned Bob down. I'm not going to do anything stupid...like getting myself killed," Bill said with a slight grin.

"Violence begets more violence, Bill; you above all people should know that. Even if you gun them down, they'll have family who'll want to see you pay for it. Then if you survive them the ones close to those you kill will come looking for you and it won't end until you're up there on the hill with Bob," Louise said in tired sounding voice.

"Well, we're all going to wind up in a grave sooner or later. I can't just walk away from Bob's murder and do nothing about it," Bill stated.

"I guess you can't, but I really wish you would. Let someone else take care of the Wrango brothers. They're bad news, Bill. Bob had a run in with them and he said that they meant trouble wherever they went," Louise said as she placed the plate of eggs and bacon in front of Bill.

Bill began to eat and Louise picked up the coffee pot and poured him a steaming hot cup of coffee. She took a couple of biscuits from the pan and placed them on his plate without saying a word.

Bill had never been close to Louise. She had been a good wife for Bob though. The two of them understood each other; something that Bill could never do; understand her.

Finally Louise broke the silence, "When will you be going into town? Do you think it will be before the stores close?" she asked.

"Yeah, I can. Why? Do you need something from the store?" Bill asked.

"I'm out of sewing thread and I noticed your shirt has a hole in it. I'll sew it up, but I need some black thread," she said.

"Okay, I'll pick some up. What about food, do you need anything?"

"No, I've got plenty. We had just bought a big bill of groceries before Bob was...," she said, not finishing the sentence.

Bill nodded in agreement, knowing she was intentionally not saying 'killed'. He hated the idea of leaving here after he'd done what he had come back to do, but knew that he'd be on the run for killing the Wrango brothers. He didn't figure on giving them a chance to draw first, that was for sure.

He finished his breakfast in silence and alone while Louise went outside to kill and pluck a chicken they would have for supper that night. Once he'd finished eating he put his plate, cup and utensils in a pan of water Louise used for washing them and went outside.

Noticing a few loose boards on the porch he took a tool box he'd found inside and began nailing the boards in place. Louise looked in his direction and smiled slightly. It was good having him around; it certainly cut the loneliness she'd felt.

18

October 13, 1879
August Wrango's ranch
20 miles out of Tucson, Arizona

Wayne Wrango looked at his brother and said angrily, "Cottonwood! Now I remember where it was I saw that jasper; Cottonwood. It was a couple of years back, remember, Hutch. We came through Cottonwood after we'd held up that freight office in Flagstaff and had a run in with two hombres in the saloon there. That's where it was that I remember that guy from…Cottonwood."

"Yeah, I remember too. Him and another fella took us for a bundle in that poker game we got in. You called him out and said he was cheatin' and we almost got in a shootout over it," Hutch said.

"He was cheatin'. No one can win the pots they were and not be cheatin'," Wayne replied.

"It couldn't be that we are just bad poker players, could it, Wayne?" Hutch replied. "When is the last time we ever walked away from a game as winners?"

"You ain't that good, but I am," Wayne snapped back.

"Oh, yeah, right...you've won so many pots I can't count 'em. You ain't no better than me and I can prove it," Hutch said.

"Then prove it," Wayne said angrily.

"Get the cards," Hutch said and pulled a wad of bills from his pocket.

Wayne grabbed a deck of cards off a table top in the parlor and carried them back to where his brother was sitting at the dinner table.

"Deal 'em," Hutch said.

"You mean you trust me to deal?"

"Yeah, you handle cards about like you handle a branding iron; not very well," Hutch laughed.

"Old Hank Acres doesn't think like that; not after I bent one over his head last week," Wayne said getting a laugh from his brother.

"Yeah, I forgot about that. Deal," Hutch repeated.

The two began to play poker and Hutch won the first three hands. When they finished the fourth game and Wayne was down twenty dollars, Hutch laughed.

"See what I mean. You're twenty dollars down and we just started."

"I'm a distance player. The longer the game goes on the more I start to win," Wayne argued.

"That is if your money holds out long enough, don't you," Hutch laughed again.

"Don't be laughing at me, Hutch. You know I don't like it when anybody laughs at me," Wayne snapped.

A Distant Thunder

Hutch laughed again which caused Wayne's neck to turn red. "I said, don't laugh at me and I mean it."

"I'll laugh at you anytime of the day or night and for as long as I want to, little brother," Hutch said as a frown came to his face.

"Laugh again and we'll see about that," Wayne said which brought a laugh from Hutch.

Wayne jumped up from his chair, knocking it over backwards in the process and leaped across the table at Hutch. The two of them crashed to the floor and began rolling around kicking and trying to hit one another. Their flailing arms and legs knocked a small table that held a lamp on it, busting it when it hit the floor.

Suddenly the door to the dining area burst open and August Wrango entered with a scowl etched on his weathered face. He had just come in through the back door of the house and was still carrying his quirt.

When he saw his two sons wrestling on the floor and tearing up the place he began to beat them both around the head and shoulders with the quirt. The two brothers stopped their fighting and covered their heads at the sting of the quirt.

"I've told you two curs about fighting in the house and tearin' up the place. Now you get up and straighten this place up or I'll use a black snake whip on you both," August said through clenched teeth.

"He started it, Pa," Wayne said, "He laughed at me."

"I'll laugh at you, you good for nothing whelp. One more time and you both will start living in the bunkhouse with the other riffraff we have working here. Now get this place cleaned up," August said as he moved away from his boys.

Wayne eyed his pa with a venomous glare until the old man was out of earshot, "One of these days I'm going to take that quirt away from him and use it on him so he sees how it feels."

"That'll be a day I don't want to miss, little brother, because that's the day you'll die," Hutch said.

"Why? Do you think I can't take the old man?"

"Oh, you can take him all right. But, you can't take both of us," Hutch said stone faced.

Wayne held his gaze on Hutch, but didn't say anything. He knew Hutch loved the old man and would, no matter what he might do to them from time to time. If he ever gunned the old man, he'd have to gun his brother too.

Tucson, Arizona

Bill Bell picked up a spool of black thread and walked up to the counter where the store clerk was standing. He looked in a glass case next to the counter and saw a pearl handled Colt .45 displayed there.

"How much do you want for the Colt .45?" Bill asked.

"That's a fine piece of hardware," the clerk stated.

"I know that; how much do you want for it?" Bell asked again, firmer this time.

"I can let you have that for $75 and it's a steal at that price," the clerk said.

"You'll let me 'have' it for $75, huh? Sounds like it would be a purchase and not a gift," Bell said tightly.

The clerk grinned awkwardly and said, "Oh, I see what you mean. Let me rephrase that. I can sell it to you for $75. I think that's a little more like, don't you Mr. Bell?"

Bell nodded ever so slightly as he said, "I'll take it...for $75."

The clerk quickly opened the locked case and removed the pistol. He started to put it in a box, but Bell stopped him.

"I don't need a box. I'm going to get used to its feel so I'll be handling it as soon as I start back to my brother's place. I'll just stick it under my belt," Bell stated.

"Oh, yes sir, Mr. Bell."

The clerk looked at the spool of thread and said, "I'm going to throw the thread into the deal and not charge you the ten cents for it."

Bell looked at the man without cracking a smile and said, "That's mighty big of you. My sister-in-law thanks you for that."

Bell took the spool of thread and stuck it in his shirt pocket. He picked up the Colt he'd just bought and stuck it in his belt and then looked at the boxes of cartridges behind the counter.

"Better give me a box of .45 caliber shells, too," he said.

"I'll tell you what I'll do," the clerk started to say.

"You're going to throw them in to sweeten the deal, also?" Bell said.

"Uh, no, uh...I was going to say I'll let you have them at half price," the clerk said.

Bell grinned to himself, "Okay, that's sweet enough for me."

Bell laid out the money for the purchases and turned to leave. The clerk cleared his throat which caused Bell to look back at him.

"I hope I'm there when you take on the Wrango boys," the clerk said.

"You won't be," Bell said and walked out of the store.

19

Bell walked down the street to the new saloon that had just completed its remodeling a few days earlier called the Crystal Palace and went inside. He took a table that faced the saloon entrance, but had his back to the wall opposite the doors.

Due to the lateness of the day the saloon was starting to fill up. It was a little more than half filled. The whir of the roulette wheel mingled with the tinkling sound of an upright piano and the murmur of the various conversations filled that area of the saloon.

A barmaid walked over to the table where Bell was seated and asked him what he wanted. He told her he just wanted a cold beer and some information. She studied his face carefully as she considered her answer.

Finally she replied, "I can help you out on the cold beer; we've got the coldest in town. As far as the information goes I'll have to wait and see what it is you want to know about."

"Do you know the Wrango brothers?" Bill asked.

The barmaid looked at him curiously before answering, "Yeah, I know them. Wayne's crazy and Hutch can be down right mean."

"Have you seen them around here today?" Bell pressed.

"No, not today and I doubt if they'll be in town anytime soon. I hear that Bill Bell is on his way back here because of the killing of his brother Bob. I don't think they want to tangle with him," the woman said.

"Is that right," Bell replied.

"You must be new in town if you didn't all ready know that," the barmaid said.

"Yeah, I must be," Bell answered.

"What's your name, honey?" she asked.

"Bell...Bill Bell," he replied which caused her to gasp slightly.

Just then Linc Sackett and Clay Butler entered the saloon, each carrying an armload of fliers about their traveling rodeo. Now that they had added another buck jumper they could handle more business and not have to worry as much about their horse wearing itself out.

"Here you go, partner," Linc said as he handed a flier to an obvious cowhand. "If you're a bronc buster you might be interested in this."

"I am a bronc buster...the best you'll ever see," the young man said.

"I'm willing to put up fifty dollars against your five that we've got two horses that you can't stay aboard for ten seconds," Linc said with a grin.

"I ain't got five dollars right now, but I will come payday," the cowboy said.

A Distant Thunder

"I'll see you payday," Linc said and moved on to another man dressed like a working hand.

Clay was also passing out fliers and explaining about the traveling rodeo and its two horses. They explained that they would only allow five riders a day for each horse. They didn't want to run the risk that one of the horses might tire and they'd be out fifty dollars. So far no rider had bested the one horse they'd been using.

When Clay approached Bill Bell's table he started to hand him a flier, but took a closer look at the man. Bell looked up into Clay's eyes and Butler knew that this man was not a bronc buster.

"I don't suppose you'd be interested in this proposition, but I'll give you a flier just the same," Clay said in a friendly tone of voice.

"What'cha got there?" Bell asked as he took the paper from Clay.

"It's about our traveling rodeo," Clay explained.

"No, I don't think I'd be interested," Bell said and handed the flier back to Butler.

"I didn't think you would," Clay grinned as he took the handbill.

"Where are you from?" Bell asked, giving Clay a long studious look.

"I lived up in the Cottonwood area for a long time, but I've been down here for sometime now. I worked on a ranch down in the area known as Tombstone now. Why do you ask?"

"You look familiar, but I guess I mistook you for someone else."

"The name is Butler if that will help jog your memory...Clay Butler."

135

"Nope, that doesn't ring a bell," Bell said and grinned and repeated quietly, "ring a bell".

Clay took on a serious look as he had a thought and asked, "You wouldn't be Bill Bell by any chance would you?"

"Yeah, I would," Bell replied.

"We heard that you might be on your way here," Clay said.

"You heard right. I came to do some business with the Wrango brothers. You don't know them I suppose?"

"It just so happens I do and it's something I'm not too proud of. In fact I had a run in with them up in Cottonwood a few years back," Clay stated.

"And you're still alive to tell about it? You must be good, Butler," Bell said with a slight grin.

"It didn't come down to a shooting; but, it got close. In fact, my partner and I saw them today out at the Double T ranch."

Bell's face tightened at Butler's comment, "So they're still in the area, huh?"

"They are," Clay replied.

"Good, I won't have to go far to find them then," Bell said as the barmaid came by with his beer.

"Join me?" Bell asked.

"I don't mind if I do," Clay said and pulled out a chair and sat down. "Bring me one of those, honey," Clay said to the barmaid.

Linc was busy handing out the fliers and hadn't seen where Clay was now seated. He made his rounds and when he finally spotted his partner walked over to the table.

"This is my partner, Linc Sackett," Clay said. "Linc, meet Bill Bell."

Linc did a double take and smiled wryly as he said, "Mr. Bell, it's nice to make your acquaintance. I would have to question your choice of drinking companions though," Linc said looking at Clay.

Linc's comment brought a chuckle for Bell as he said, "Won't you join us?"

The three men got along well together, each having a good understanding of the other. After a couple of beers, Linc and Clay excused themselves and explained that they had to finish handing out the handbills if they were going to make any money.

Bell liked the two men he'd just met. He hadn't had time to meet a lot of men he would feel comfortable calling 'friend', but he felt he could do that with these two.

Bell had been forced into being living a life as a gunfighter. He'd gotten into an argument with two men while in Lordsburg ten years earlier and there was a shootout. Bell had wounded one man seriously and killed the other man. The other man turned out to be a fast gun around the Lordsburg area and Bell's reputation built up from there.

It seemed that every one horse town he went into had a gunny who wanted to make a name for himself and Bell was forced to kill again. He longed for a life of peace and quiet, but trouble was always just around the corner, it seemed. Going against the Wrango's would only add to his growing reputation.

Bell was just finishing his beer when Crystal Bell walked up to his table. He hadn't seen her approaching and looked up quickly when she stopped across the table from him.

"Hello Bill," Crystal said with a slight smile.

"Crystal...what are you doing here?" Bill said in a shocked voice.

20

"I own this place," Crystal said looking around the large saloon.

"The Crystal Palace, I didn't even consider that you might have something to do with this place," Bill stated.

Crystal looked caringly at Bill as she asked, "How've you been?"

"You know me, fine as frog's hair. It looks like you're doing good for yourself. I'm glad," Bill said honestly.

"I've thought of you often and wondered if our paths would ever cross again. I'm sorry about Bob. I guess that's why you're here, huh?" Crystal said.

Bill nodded his head slowly, "Yeah, I can't let this pass without payback."

"When will it stop, Bill? When someone beats you to the draw and you wind up lying face down on some muddy street somewhere?"

Bill nodded slowly, "Probably."

"Don't you want to stop?"

"You don't know how much I want to, but I can't. I guess the only way out of this life will be feet first," Bill said.

"I've missed you...missed you terribly," Crystal said honestly.

"And I've missed you...terribly," Bill replied and then added. "When did you get into the saloon business? I figured you would still be teaching school somewhere."

"It was quite by accident, I can tell you that. I met and fell for a gambling man. He showed me how to play poker and I found that I not only liked it, but I was very good at it.

"Well, one thing led to another and the next thing you know I was running a poker parlor in Amarillo, Texas. From there I moved to El Paso, but was forced to leave there.

"My business partner and I made a bid on this place when it was auctioned off and got it. It looks like it's going to be a successful venture," Crystal explained.

Bill nodded his head as she talked and when she finished said, "You always did have a good head on your pretty shoulders."

Crystal smiled and grew silent for a moment before saying, "Who are these Wrango brothers who shot Bob?"

"They're scum. They've bushwhacked more people for no reason than any two men I've ever heard of. They shot one man because he caused one of the brothers to spill his drink.

"I really don't know what the trouble between them and Bob was about. It doesn't really matter to me, I guess. I just know that they have to pay for what they did and unless I make them pay up, no one will," Bill said tightly.

"I wanted to go out and see Louise, but I just didn't have the heart to face her. There were hard feelings because I left here after you headed for Texas. How is she?" Crystal said solemnly.

"She's dealing with Bob's death okay, I guess. Louise has never been an easy woman to get close too. I sure can't understand her and I know why you feel the way you do about her. She was good for Bob though," Bill answered.

"She probably doesn't even know I'm back in these parts; and probably doesn't care. If it should come up, I hope you will tell her that I asked about her," Crystal said.

"I will," Bill said.

Just then one of the floor men came over to the table and cleared his throat.

"Yeah, Jim, what is it?" Crystal asked.

"We have a guy at the roulette table who wants to raise the limit. What do you say?" the man asked.

"How much does he want to raise it?" Crystal asked.

"He wants to bet two thousand dollars."

"Has he been lucky?" Crystal asked.

"No, not really," the man said.

"Then raise it," she said and looked at Bill.

Bill had to smile at the craftiness of Crystal. She had always been so savvy about things. She just seemed to always know what to do or say for any given situation.

"I'd better got check this out, Bill," Crystal said as she got up from the seat she'd taken earlier.

Raymond D. Mason

"I understand. I'll probably see you around. I'll be here a few days, I'm sure," Bill said.

"I hope so, Bill. Take care, please," Crystal said and turned and walked away.

Bill watched her walk away from him and felt a twinge of loneliness in his heart. He'd loved Crystal from the first time he had laid eyes on her. There brief marriage had ended badly because of a couple of shootings he could not avoid.

He was stunned that Crystal was the owner of a saloon. She wouldn't even take a drink of whiskey during the two years they were married and now she was selling it.

Bill watched her for a few minutes and then got up and walked out of the saloon. When he got to his horse he took the new gun he'd bought and loaded it. He wanted to shoot it and get a feel for it and figured he'd have a chance as he headed back to Bob's place.

When he found a lonely spot along the road he took the gun out of his belt and hefted it to get a good feel for its balance. Looking towards a small cactus he took his other pistol from his holster and slipped the new Colt into it.

Bell took his stance and stood in a relaxed position for a moment before drawing the pistol with lightning quick speed and firing; hitting the cactus dead center.

He mounted up again and rode back to Bob's place. After he'd taken care of his horse for the night Bell headed for the house. Seeing an axe lying on the ground he picked it up and swung it with one hand, sticking it in a small log to be used for firewood.

Due to the darkness and the location Bill had not seen the two horses that were tied up in back of the house. The horses belonged to none other than Hutch and Wayne Wrango.

Bill opened the door and saw Louise seated in a chair with a tense look on her face. He started to say something when suddenly the door was slammed into him, knocking him down.

Hutch Wrango had been hiding behind the door with Wayne hiding in the next room where he could see the front door. Neither of the men saw the new Colt .45 Bill had bought when it was knocked from under his belt and slid under a chair.

Hutch held his pistol in Bill's face as he laughed hideously. Wayne rushed into the room and he too giggled like a crazy man.

"Well, looky here, Wayne," Hutch said pointing the gun at Bell, "we've got us a rough, tough fast gun."

"He don't look all that rough, tough, or fast to me. He looks plum scared if you want to know the truth," Wayne replied.

"Are you all right, Louise?" Bill asked from his position on the floor.

"Yes, Bill; they haven't hurt me. They just got here about ten minutes ago," Louise said.

"Shut up you two," Hutch snapped angrily.

"Why don't you do what you're going to do to me and let her go," Bell said with a deep frown.

Raymond D. Mason

"Shut up, just shut up. We'll do what we want and take our own sweet time in doing it," Hutch snapped angrily.

"You're both good for nothing dung heaps," Bell said, spitting the words from his mouth.

Hutch kicked Bell in the stomach, knocking the wind out of him and laughed as he said, "You're the one rolling around on the floor, gunfighter. Let's see you shoot your way out of this."

Finally getting his wind back, Bell looked to his left and saw the new Colt under the chair about five feet away from where he lay. He didn't want to tip his hand too soon in going for the gun for fear they would beat him to it.

Bell slowly pulled himself to his hands and knees and began crawling slowly in the direction of the chair, but acting as though it was to get away from Hutch.

"Oh, no you don't, gunfighter," Hutch said and kicked him again, knocking him even closer to the chair.

Hutch had done exactly what Bell had hoped he would do. As he lunged forward from the force of the blow, he was able to slide his hand under the chair without drawing any attention to what he was going for.

Wayne had moved around so he was standing alongside his brother and they both glared down at the seemingly helpless Bell. Feeling the pistol grip firmly in his hand Bell pulled his hand out from under the chair and cocked the hammer back as he leveled it at Hutch.

A Distant Thunder

The roar from the Colt was deafening in the confined space of the small front room. The bullet hit Hutch in the middle of the chest, knocking him backwards about four feet.

Wayne was shocked at the suddenness of the change of events and stood frozen with his eyes wide open. The next shot from the Colt hit him in near the heart. He fell to the floor with a dull thud; he too was dead.

Bell slowly got to his feet although listing to one side where he had been kicked. He looked down at the two dead Wrango brothers, but felt no real satisfaction in the fact he had killed them.

Bell looked from the gore of the kill to his sister-in-law and asked, "Are you all right?"

"Yes, Bill I am. Let me look at your ribs. They may be broken," Louise said caringly.

It was the first time Bell had ever heard such tenderness come from his sister-in-law and it made him smile weakly. She checked his ribs and could feel that two of them were busted.

After wrapping large bandages around Bell's chest, Louise started trying to move the bodies of the two brothers outside the house. Bell wanted to help, but found it too difficult with the broken ribs.

"Ride into town and get the temporary sheriff, Louise. I'll be all right," Bill said.

"Okay, if you're sure you'll be okay," she replied.

Bell nodded and said he would be. Louise saddled her horse and headed off into the night to fetch the temporary sheriff the town had appointed until one could be formally selected by the town council until a proper election was held.

The acting sheriff was savvy enough to bring the undertaker with him and they carted the Wrango brother's into Tucson to the funeral parlor. The sheriff said he would ride out the next day and inform old man Wrango of his two son's deaths.

Bill Bell feared that the blood feud would continue. He had seen these things before and they only seemed to escalate in scope and intensity. He told Louise that once his ribs had healed enough for him to ride, he'd be moving on.

He really didn't think old man Wrango would hold anything against Louise. After all, it wasn't her who had shot and killed his boys. No, he would be looking to even the score with Bill Bell.

21

The Sackett Ranch
October 14, 1879
Abilene, Texas

Brian Sackett rode up to the front of his pa's house and sat astraddle his horse for a few moments to collect his thoughts as to what he was about to say. It wasn't going to be easy, but he felt it was something he had to do.

He stepped off his mount and tied the reins to the hitching rail. He looked again at the house and took a deep breath before starting his walk up the walkway to the front steps.

John and AJ Sackett were having breakfast in the kitchen with the women of the household and hadn't been aware that Brian had ridden up. He stopped at the door not knowing whether he should knock or just go on in like he'd always done before.

He decided to just go on inside and get off his chest what he had to say. Brian knew that he'd been wrong in the way he'd handled his crisis. He should have talked it over with his pa and brother.

Raymond D. Mason

A little pride had held him back from doing so, however. After all, they'd heard him making comments about getting married.

The family all looked up when Brian walked into the kitchen and nodded his greeting to them; his hat in his hands. John could tell something was brewing, but figured to let Brian speak first.

"Hi," Brian said shyly.

"Hey, little brother, you're just in time for breakfast," AJ said quickly as he smiled at Brian.

"I've already eaten...thanks. I just stopped by to tell you all I'm leaving this area. I think I'll head out to California and see if I can hook up with Brent," Brian said in a tight, but soft voice.

John didn't say a word, just stared at his youngest son searching for the right words to say. Brian went on, "I want to apologize for the way I was acting, but it was something that no one could help me with and I had to work things out in my own mind."

"Hey, that's all water under the bridge now, Brian," AJ replied quickly.

"Well, that may be true, but it's a bridge I want to get as far away from as I can because of my feelings," Brian answered.

"It can't be that bad," AJ argued.

"Maybe not to some, but it is to me. You see, I was planning on asking Terrin to marry me, but I guess you all figured that out sometime ago. Well, it turns out that she doesn't have the same feelings for me that I have for her.

"The truth is that she was in love with the banker who was killed in that bank holdup down in Buffalo Gap last week," Brian confessed.

John nodded his head and finally spoke, "And you believe you'll be reminded too much of her if you stay around here; is that it?"

"Yeah, Pa, I guess that's it. I think I just need to get away for awhile and let my head clear up. I've thought it over and I want to find Brent. Don't ask me why or how, but I think I can help him out of the mess he's gotten himself into," Brian said.

"Brian, you're a grown man and you've got a mind of your own, so I won't try to stop you from doing what you believe you have to do. Personally, I think you're wrong. I've found that hard work helps a man forget his past troubles faster than anything, but that's just my way of thinking.

"You do what you think you must. The ranch will still be here if you ever decide you want to come back. If not...well, all I can say is 'good luck'. I hope you've thought this out real good, though," John said solemnly.

Mrs. Sackett spoke at this time, "Brian, son, please don't go. You'll find someone else to marry. I know how much you loved Terrin, but things have a way of working out if you'll just give them time."

"Thanks Ma, but my mind is made up I'm afraid. Don't worry, though; I'll write you and keep you up to date on where I am and what I'm doing," Brian said.

Brian nodded his head slowly at his pa's words. He looked at the faces of his sisters' and at AJ's. He walked over to his mother and kissed her on the forehead. He went to each sister and did the same thing. When he had worked his way around to AJ, AJ stood up and the two brothers embraced one another in a brotherly hug.

Brian turned to John and stuck out his hand. John looked at Brian's outstretched hand and stood up. He shook Brian's hand, but then hugged his youngest boy.

"God go with you, Son," John said. "Let us know where you light."

"I will Pa; I promise," Brian said and looked around the table at the gathering of those he loved.

"I'll miss you all," he said and turned around quickly and left before they could see the tears forming in his eyes.

Brian hurried down the steps and out to where his horse was tied. He didn't take time to say goodbye to any of the ranch hands. All he wanted to do was get on the trail; the trail to forgetfulness.

He mounted up and headed in the direction of Abilene. When Brian reached the end of the corral he turned in the saddle and gave the ranch house one last look. He knew his life was taking another major turn. He only hoped it was for the best; but, only time would tell if that was to be the case or not.

"California, ready or not, you'll soon have two Sackett's to deal with," Brian said under his breath.

The End

Look for the next book in the Sackett series:
'Dark Moon Rider'

A Distant Thunder

Books by This Author

Mysteries

8 Seconds to Glory - A Motive for Murder - A Tale of Tri-Cities - A Walk on the Wilder Side – Beyond Missing - Blossoms in the Dust - Brotherhood of the Cobra – Counterfeit Elvis: Welcome to My World – Corrigan - If Looks Could Kill - Illegal Crossing - In the Chill of the Night - Most Deadly Intentions – Murder on the Oregon Express - Odor in the Court - On a Lonely Mountain Road - Return of 'Booger' Doyle - Send in the Clones - Shadows of Doubt - Sleazy Come, Sleazy Go - Suddenly, Murder - The Mystery of Myrtle Creek - The Secret of Spirit Mountain - The Tootsie Pop Kid - The Woman in the Field – Too Late To Live

Westerns

Aces and Eights - Across the Rio Grande – A Distant Thunder - American Knights: Miles Knight - Between Heaven and Hell - Beyond the Great Divide - Beyond the Picket Wire - Brimstone; End of the Trail - Day of the Rawhiders - Four Corners Woman – Guns of Vengeance Valley - Incident at Medicine Bow - King of the Barbary Coast - Laramie - Last of the Long Riders - Man from Silver City – Moon Stalker - Night of the Blood Red Moon - Night Riders - Purple Dawn - Rage at Del Rio - Range War - Rebel Pride - Return to Cutter's Creek - Ride the Hard Land - Ride the Hellfire Trail - Showdown at Lone Pine - Streets of Durango: *Lynching* - Streets of Durango: *Shootings* - Tales of Old Arizona - The Long Ride Back - Three Days to Sundown - Yellow Sky, Black Hawk

Mystery Series

Dan Wilder Series:
A Walk on the Wilder Side – Send in the Clones – Murder on the Oregon Express – A Tale of Tri-Cities – Odor in the Court

Nick Castle Series:

Raymond D. Mason

Brotherhood of the Cobra – Beyond Missing – Suddenly, Murder

Frank Corrigan Series:
Corrigan – Shadows of Doubt – Return of Booger Doyle

Western Books Series (In Sequential Order)

Quirt Adams Series:
The Long Ride Back – Return to Cutter's Creek – Ride the Hellfire Trail – Brimstone: End of the Trail – Night Riders

Sackett Series:
Across the Rio Grande – Three Days to Sundown - Ride the Hard Land – Range War – Five Faces West – Between Heaven and Hell – Guns of Vengeance Valley

Luke Sanders Series:
Day of the Rawhiders – Moon Stalker

Streets of Durango Series:
Streets of Durango: the lynching – Streets of Durango: the shootings

For paperback books go to www.createspace.com and use L9ZJ9ZJJ for 'discount code' to save 30%.

All of Raymond D. Mason's books are on Kindle.

A Distant Thunder

Raymond D. Mason

Printed in Great Britain
by Amazon